LOVE
FROM A STRANGER

Leslie's heart was in turmoil as she drove alone through the night. Donald Shaw, the intense, craggy-faced newcomer, filled her thoughts. There was so much that was puzzling about him—the veil of suspicion that surrounded his work at the Clayton plant; the strange resemblance he bore to Douglas Clayton, the brilliant young heir—missing and presumed dead in combat. Leslie really knew nothing about Donald except that she loved him. That day he'd begged her to trust him, *no matter what happened.* "Why?" she wondered as she drove down the lonely stretch of country road.

Then, suddenly, the headlights of her car illuminated two figures locked in an embrace at the side of the road. In the vivid glare, Leslie recognized glamorous Felice Allen . . . and Donald.

A CANDLE IN HER HEART

Books by Emilie Loring

- FOR ALL YOUR LIFE
- WHAT THEN IS LOVE
- I TAKE THIS MAN
- MY DEAREST LOVE
- LOOK TO THE STARS
- BEHIND THE CLOUD
- THE SHADOW OF SUSPICION
- WITH THIS RING
- BEYOND THE SOUND OF GUNS
- HOW CAN THE HEART FORGET
- TO LOVE AND TO HONOR
- LOVE CAME LAUGHING BY
- I HEAR ADVENTURE CALLING
- THROW WIDE THE DOOR
- BECKONING TRAILS
- BRIGHT SKIES
- THERE IS ALWAYS LOVE
- STARS IN YOUR EYES
- KEEPERS OF THE FAITH
- WHERE BEAUTY DWELLS
- FOLLOW YOUR HEART
- RAINBOW AT DUSK
- WHEN HEARTS ARE LIGHT AGAIN
- TODAY IS YOURS
- ACROSS THE YEARS

- Published by Bantam Books, Inc.

EMILIE LORING

A CANDLE
IN
HER HEART

BANTAM BOOKS · TORONTO · NEW YORK · LONDON

*The names of all characters in this novel
are fictitious. If the name of any living
person has been used it is coincidence.*

*This low-priced Bantam Book
has been completely reset in a type face
designed for easy reading, and was printed
from new plates. It contains the complete
text of the original hard-cover edition.*
NOT ONE WORD HAS BEEN OMITTED.

A CANDLE IN HER HEART
*A Bantam Book / published by arrangement with
Little, Brown and Company*

PRINTING HISTORY
*Little, Brown edition published March 1964
Bantam edition published March 1967*

Published simultaneously in the United States and Canada.

*Bantam Books are published by Bantam Books, Inc., a subsidiary
of Grosset & Dunlap, Inc. Its trade-mark, consisting of the words
"Bantam Books" and the portrayal of a bantam, is registered in the
United States Patent Office and in other countries. Marca Registrada.
Bantam Books, Inc., 271 Madison Avenue, New York, N.Y. 10016.*

PRINTED IN THE UNITED STATES OF AMERICA

"HOW MUCH longer," the man asked impatiently, "is this to go on?"

Dr. John Forsyth studied his patient. There was a faintly Mephistophelean cast to the famous doctor's features, emphasized by the small pointed beard, the triangular peak of black eyebrows. At the moment, a sardonic look of amusement on his face increased the impression.

He got to his feet. It's over—as of now. I've done my best for you." With a swift gesture, like a conjurer, he flung open the two folding sides of a full-length mirror and stood back.

"Well, how do you like yourself, Donald Shaw?"

The patient stood up slowly, as though bracing himself for a shock. "Donald Shaw," he said in a thoughtful tone. "I've got to get used to that. It—"

He caught sight of the man in the mirror and broke off sharply. The man in the mirror repeated his involuntary step backward, stared at him with shocked, unbelieving eyes. He was a tall man in his early thirties, broad-shouldered, lean-hipped, with thick dark hair cut very short and neatly parted on one side. There were unexpected patches of white above his ears. Startled gray eyes looked back from a thin face. A resolute chin was balanced by the sensitivity of the mouth. It would have been a singularly handsome face if it had not looked so grim.

When at last he spoke his voice was shaken. "I look like a man who has just climbed out of hell."

"That's about what you have done," Dr. Forsyth told him, his tone so matter-of-fact that his patient relaxed, though he still continued to stare in incredulous fascination at his own face.

"I'll be lucky if I don't scare small children into nightmares," he said, trying to laugh.

"When you stop feeling grim you'll stop looking grim,"

the doctor said. "After all, this was your own idea, you know. You brought it on yourself. It's rather late in the day to find that you have any regrets."

"No," the man called Shaw said quietly. "No regrets."

"Take it all in all," Forsyth said, "you could get by anywhere without arousing any comment, any question, except—"

"Well?"

"There are, of course, a lot of—signs of what has happened to you. I think you'd be wise to keep out of strong sunlight and I'd advise you not to go swimming, unless you can prepare yourself with a convincing story."

Shaw turned away from the mirror as though dismissing his image from his mind. He held out his hand. "Doctor, I can't begin to tell you—"

"There's no need," Forsyth assured him as they shook hands. "It has been a most interesting and rewarding experiment for me. The important thing now is, how much money do you have left?"

Shaw grinned at him. "Enough."

"Of course, you'll let me help when you run short."

Shaw held up his hand in protest. "No," he said firmly. "You've done enough. No one else could have done or would have attempted to do a tenth of what you have done for me." The sensitive mouth twisted in a grimace. "There must have been many times during this interminable ordeal when you wondered whether there was any point in going on."

The doctor's eyes were on his patient's face. "Is that the way you felt about it?"

"At first, yes. It seemed so hopeless. But when I stopped feeling sorry for myself I began to realize what you were doing for me. After that, the struggle was worthwhile. The fact that there were people like you made it worthwhile."

Dr. Forsyth hastily dismissed any discussion of the assistance he had given the young man.

"Nearly anyone," he said, "would have regarded it as the inadequate payment of a great debt. In any case, that's the past. Let's forget it. What counts is the future. How do you expect to live if you stick to this insane idea of yours?"

Shaw reached for his wallet, pulled out a small newspaper clipping. It was an advertisement for experimental chemists to work at the Clayton Textile Company at Claytonville, Connecticut.

Dr. Forsyth read it slowly, returned it. "Isn't that rather risky?"

For the first time Shaw smiled, an engaging smile that

lighted the grim face, that made the man likable and irresistibly attractive. "I've taken other risks."

"God knows you have!" the doctor said fervently. He added, "I wish I knew what you are up to, why you are doing this."

The younger man made no reply. He sat on the edge of the desk, lighting a cigarette, his gray eyes, which were so warm when he smiled, now cold and bleak.

"From the beginning," the doctor protested, his face troubled, "I have been opposed to the whole idea. I don't know why I ever let you talk me into it. But you were so determined and, what with one thing and another, I didn't want to argue about it."

"One thing and another!" Shaw laughed softly. "Well, I must get busy now."

"At least, tell me what you plan to do, beyond going to Douglas Clayton's home town and trying to land a job in his company."

"Douglas Clayton is dead," Shaw said quietly. "He died in Korea years ago. And his—"

"By the way," Forsyth interrupted, "did you ever see an old documentary war film of the Tower Heights offensive?"

"No!" Shaw was startled.

"It might interest you. I noticed in the morning's paper that it is being shown at that old-film theater on Fiftieth Street. Last time Clayton was ever seen alive. His stature as a hero has grown so much over the years that the film is being shown again by popular demand."

"Well, I'll be darned. I'll see it this afternoon."

"And after that?" the doctor persisted.

"After that—well, I've applied for that chemist's job. There's a reason for it. The chief thing is that I'd like to see how sound the company is, how it is being handled."

"You're holding out on me," the doctor accused him. When Shaw made no reply, Forsyth said slowly, "I don't know much about the outfit. Of course, Corliss Blake inherited it when Douglas Clayton was missing, presumed dead, in Korea. So far as I know, he's a good man. He's not a chemist, and he was such a distant relation, third or fourth cousin, I think, and so much older than Clayton, that he never expected to inherit."

"What else do you know about him?"

"His wife—his first wife, that is—died when his only child, a daughter named Leslie, was born. The story is that he never got over it. He remarried, about a year later."

"Then what do you mean, he never got over it?" Shaw asked in amusement.

"Well, the second marriage, as far as I can make out, wasn't a love match. Not by a long shot. Agatha Winslow. Tremendously wealthy woman."

"Oh." Shaw was thoughtfully silent.

"Blake may have had his eye on her money but he seems to be running the Clayton plant all right." Forsyth was answering Shaw's tone, the speculation in his voice. "He's honest enough, so far as I've learned. I've heard rumors that they are working on a new kind of textile, a secret formula, revolutionary by all reports. They might be on to something big. I don't know."

The doctor studied the younger man's brooding expression. "I wish," he began abruptly. Stopped. He added casually, though it wasn't what he had started to say, "By the way, the girl Douglas Clayton was engaged to at the time of his death is still living in Claytonville. She married a local man named Williams. John Williams. Well-heeled but considerably older than she was. He died a couple of years ago. She has a son Jack, nine years old."

"Nine years. Apparently she didn't mourn Clayton very long." Shaw went to the window and stood looking out on Park Avenue. He spoke without turning around. "Spring loses its magic in New York. It will be good to live in the country for a change."

"Perhaps that is what you need," Dr. Forsyth told him. "A little spring magic."

"That comes only once," Shaw said quietly.

"Nonsense!" The doctor addressed Shaw's back, his voice brisk and professional. "It comes every year. But you have to know how to recognize it, how to welcome it."

Shaw turned around. To the doctor's relief, he was smiling. "You're a very wise man." He laid his hand lightly on the doctor's shoulder, then turned toward the door.

"Where are you going?"

Shaw grinned at him. "I'm going to look for spring," he said, flipped his hand in a gay little salute and went out of the office, closing the door firmly behind him.

*   *   *

Even in the heart of Manhattan there were hints of early summer. Shaw strode rapidly along Park Avenue, turned west and waited for a green light so he could cross the street. Men were carrying their topcoats over their arms, women had changed from dark winter clothing to light dresses, and sauntered, pausing to look at the shop windows. Tufts of cloud scudded across a deep blue sky.

Shaw walked to Fifth Avenue and into Central Park. Small boys wobbled past uncertainly on bicycles or sprawled on the grass. Children, he thought, knew how to welcome the coming of summer, knew how to respond to it.

On benches in the sun a couple of elderly men read newspapers and rejoiced in the beneficent season's warmth. A middle-aged woman was feeding squirrels from a bag of peanuts. When they had whisked off with the peanuts stuffed in their cheeks, she sat in placid contentment, watching the slow progress of the man with the balloons, the dazzling reflections of the sun on the higher windows of apartment buildings on Central Park West.

A young couple strolled along the path, their arms around each other, as isolated as though they were on a desert island. For them life was at its radiant beginning. Watching them, Donald Shaw was aware of loneliness. It was as though a black cloud had covered the sun even while it continued to shine as brightly as before, casting its light and its warmth on everything but the tall man who walked alone under the trees with their shiny new leaves.

Like a man in flight, trying to escape from himself, Shaw took the first path that would lead him back to Fifth Avenue, back to the safe anonymity of a great city. Far downtown he could see the shining tower of the Empire State Building, and, closer to him, the great shafts of Rockefeller Center reaching up into the sky. Beside him there was the ceaseless roar and movement of traffic, buses, taxis, every possible variety of car from tiny Volkswagens to long sleek chauffeur-driven Lincolns and Rolls-Royces.

As he continued to walk south, with no particular destination in mind, he left the park behind, and passed the shop windows below Fifty-ninth Street. Deep in his thoughts, he was unaware of the people who turned for a second look at him. Men observed enviously his lithe carriage, the proud bearing of his head, the unstressed authority he wore like a coat, and thought he must be someone of importance. Women's eyes lingered wistfully on his face, wondering who he was.

Through his absorption in his thoughts there crept an increasing awareness that he was tired. He had been walking for more than two hours. How long was it, he wondered, since he had walked so far? But this, at least, was healthy fatigue. Tonight, he might be able to sleep soundly, to sleep without nightmares.

He had to rest. No point in overdoing it on his first day of real freedom. He looked at a street sign. He was at Fiftieth Street. His hesitation was only momentary. After all, why not? He had to admit to himself that he was curious. He turned west, looking for the movie theater. He saw the sign: *The Tower Heights Offensive.* He bought a ticket and went inside.

The theater was small, only one floor. Now, in the late afternoon, it was nearly empty. Even before he looked at the screen he heard the sounds of battle, the rattle of machine-gun fire, the long scream and explosion of a shell. Instinctively, he ducked, and then grinned wryly to himself.

The screen was gray. It was hard to distinguish what was going on in the dim light. Little by little, he could make out American Infantry moving cautiously across a plain. It was halted by fire from the Heights. Suddenly, through a silver mist of dust, a man emerged, a tall man, haggard, with sunken eyes.

He turned, shouting, his revolver in his hand. He was pushing his way among the men. He was out of sight. Then he emerged again, alone now, moving up the side of the hill. There was a barrage of fire and he dropped. Then he was moving again, crawling, clawing his way up the hill toward the hidden machine-gun nest.

The troops in the foreground were scattering, trying to escape the relentless fire from the enemy over the crest of the hill. The crawling man was nearly at the top now, taking advantage of every rock, every bit of cover he could find. Beside him there was an explosion. The ground seemed to blow apart. For a moment dust concealed him. No, he was moving again. One hand groped around, found a rock, pulled feebly. Stopped. Tried again. Inch by inch, he dragged himself, always moving toward the enemy. A final pull. He was over the crest. Out of sight.

There were shots. A strange silence. Nothing moved. Then a cheer rocked the troops in the foreground, they rallied, began a concerted rush up the side of the hill.

The screen was suddenly blank and white. The small audience stirred, women powdered their noses and gathered up their packages. Men reached for cigarettes, prepared to light up in the lobby.

Donald Shaw went slowly up the aisle, and out onto the street. Twilight had fallen. There was a red glow in the west. New York was a blaze of light. For a moment, Shaw paused uncertainly until he became aware that impatient, hurrying New Yorkers were bumping into him, shoving past him. He walked to the curb and hailed a passing cab.

"Grand Central Station," he said.

It was still commuting time when he reached the station. He stood at the top of the wide flight of stairs on the

Vanderbilt Avenue side, looking at the mammoth lighted advertising signs and at the scurrying throngs below who were racing for the various tracks, at the lines formed at a dozen ticket windows, at redcaps weighted down under suitcases or pushing handtrucks piled high with luggage.

He made his way through the crowds to a ticket window, bought a ticket to Claytonville, Connecticut.

"Round trip?" the ticket agent asked without looking at the purchaser.

"One way." Donald Shaw pocketed the ticket and his change with an oddly excited feeling of finality. There was to be no turning back now.

"Next train in an hour and a half," he was told. "You just missed one."

An hour and a half. Now what? Dinner, perhaps? Shaw paused to consider, ran the fingers of his left hand through his hair, a gesture so automatic that he had become unconscious of it. He had been dimly aware that behind him two girls were chattering eagerly. One of them gasped, whispered.

Unexpectedly, a hand touched his arm, a girl cried out on a note of incredulous delight: "Douglas Clayton!"

He wheeled around. The girl, no hat on her short copper curls, big brown eyes wide with shock, dropped her hand as though she had burned it on his sleeve.

"Sorry," she whispered. "My mistake."

She backed away from him uncertainly, the warm color sweeping in a tide over her face.

As the two girls walked quickly toward the information desk, he stood looking after them. He tried to light a cigarette and discovered that his hands were shaking.

LESLIE BLAKE opened her eyes, saw the sunlight in a wide golden path across the carpet, and got out of bed. She thrust small feet into satin mules the color of Killarney roses at their deepest, threw a filmy negligee of a slightly warmer hue over her shoulders, and went to look out of the window and welcome the morning.

She drew a long breath. The air was spicy with the wet breath of firs and balsams. The glistening stepping stones of a prim path led from the warm red brick of the house to an opening in a hedge flushed with rhododendrons, dripping with snowy bridal wreath, fragrant with waxy syringa. On the smooth emerald of the lawn a robin strutted haughtily, looked round him in disdain, and lifted his voice in his morning chant. Pines and spruce towered against a sunwashed sky. The lawn sloped down to the river, sparkling in the sun, with a thousand spangles dancing on it.

The only flaw in the scene was a battered-up old barge, moored to heavy stakes on the bank. Leslie made a face at it.

"Your days are numbered. Sometime I'll get rid of you, you old eyesore, if it's the last thing I ever do."

She dressed in pale green, brushed the soft curls until there were splinters of copper light in them, and ran down the stairs. Her father and stepmother were already in the breakfast room, and the glow faded from the girl's face as she heard her stepmother laying down the law as usual in a long monologue, punctuated at intervals by a monosyllabic comment from her patient husband.

Corliss Blake didn't, Leslie thought, look like the kind of man who could be bossed by women. He was heavy-set, his brown hair lightly streaked with gray. Shaggy brows hung over his eyes like thatch from the edge of a country roof. A Roman nose and a jutting chin gave his face a touch of belligerence.

His wife, whom Leslie called "Aunt Agatha" because she couldn't bring herself to say "Mother" to her father's second wife, was an ox-eyed Juno, a large phlegmatic woman, handsome but without charm, well meaning but insensitive who went through life like a steam roller, trampling on people's feelings without the slightest awareness of what she was doing.

The chief difficulty in coping with Agatha Blake was that, invariably, she meant well. It wasn't fair to be driven half mad with annoyance against a woman whose intentions were always good, who took a stern pride in being unselfish but never failed to let the hapless recipient of her heavy-handed kindness know it.

For a moment Leslie paused in the breakfast room doorway. The sun streamed through a great window with many panes, shone through a collection of choice glass arranged on a narrow shelf against it: a piece of clear lemon-yellow; a curious mauve-tinted flagon; green bottles, a pair of them; bits of amber, pink, crimson, transformed by the sunlight into gleaming jewels.

She slipped into her place at the table. "Good morning, Dad. Good morning, Aunt Agatha. What a glorious day! Nothing to mar it but that dingy old barge. Sooner or later," she added darkly, "I'm going to set fire to the ugly thing."

Her father gave her a quick look from under his shaggy eyebrows. "The barge stays where it is," he said. "I don't want to hear any more about it, Leslie."

"But it's such an eyesore," she began in protest.

"I must say," Agatha put in, "I agree with Leslie about that hideous barge. If we could just get rid of it, we could have a really attractive small dock and a nice diving board. After all, Corliss, this is your property to do with as you see fit."

"After all," he broke in with a tone of authority he rarely used either to his wife or his daughter, "the barge belonged to Douglas Clayton. It was his favorite playground as a small boy. He dived from it and fished and played pirate. While I live, it will remain where it is, untouched."

"Really, my dear," Agatha protested, "you are rather absurd at times about the Clayton boy, because you inherited the money and the business and this house; sheer chance, after all."

"Not sheer chance, Agatha. Douglas Clayton sacrificed his life magnificently. All this—the business, the money, the house. But more. Much more. Another forty years of life, perhaps. Time for a happy marriage and children of his own. Time to find where his abilities lay and to develop them. Time for a rich and fruitful middle age and mellow years of fulfillment. Time to dream dreams and watch them come true. Time for the seasons as they unfold."

He broke off, cleared his throat. "Everything we have today we owe to Douglas Clayton. The barge stays where it is, Leslie."

"Of course," she said quietly, "I hadn't thought of it like that."

So far as Agatha was concerned, her husband might as well not have spoken. "I must repeat," she said in her flat voice, "I think you are rather absurd about the Clayton boy. That memorial festival you are planning for him on the Green, for instance. After all, millions of young men have died in battle. That didn't make them necessarily all heroes. And one thing you seem to forget; you don't owe *everything* to Douglas Clayton. After all, I have my own money and you know I'm always glad to let you have what you want."

"How well I know." Corliss Blake bit off the words, got up to kiss his wife lightly on the forehead and smiled at Leslie. "I must be off."

"So early?" Agatha protested. "In your position you don't need to get to work at this hour. After all, you owe it to your own dignity and your status to go in at a later time."

"I have some young chemists to interview. There have been a number of applications and we are still weeding out the applicants. Only three left to choose among and two of them will be in today."

"But you are no chemist yourself," Agatha pointed out. "You are hardly equipped to decide about their qualifications. Why don't you simply leave the decision to Oliver Harrison? Dear Oliver is always so ready and willing to help."

Leslie pleated her napkin in her lap, her soft full lips pressed firmly together. How could her father bear it? How could he maintain his eternal patience when Agatha interfered with everything?

"I left the chemical end to Oliver," he said tranquilly. "But the essential thing is to select a trustworthy man. It's character we need, over and above ability. If a competing firm were to get hold of the new formula—and the Gypton Company, at any rate, would go to any lengths, pay any price, it would be a tremendous blow to us."

"I'm glad you have Oliver," Agatha said. "Now there's a man with a future, if I ever saw one." She turned to Leslie. "You haven't asked him to dinner for weeks. Any time you want to have him, you know, I'd be simply delighted."

"Thank you." Leslie's hands clenched into small fists. If only Agatha wouldn't try to run everything! Now she was determined to marry Leslie off suitably. If there were only some way she could support herself, be independent, free from Agatha's domination, the everlasting clink of Agatha's money. At least, she could do something productive.

"Dad," she said impulsively, and her father stopped at the door. Looked back.

"Yes, dear?"

"Is there any reason why I couldn't work on a statue of Douglas Clayton for the Green?"

"I don't see why you shouldn't try it if you would like to."

"Don't you think," Agatha pointed out, "it would be better if you didn't? In a way it would be absurd to try it. There are so many professional sculptors."

Corliss gave his wife a quick look, turned to Leslie. "Doing creative work of some kind, any kind, whether it's making a fireplace bench or landscaping a garden, is necessary if a person is to be complete. I'd be delighted to have you go back to sculpting." He smiled at his daughter.

"How can I find out what he looked like? Are there any pictures of him here in the house?"

"No, I understand he gave them all to Jane Williams— Jane Brooke, she was then—when he became engaged to her. She may have kept them."

Again Corliss Blake started toward the door. Again he turned back. "Oh, there's a theater in New York showing *The Tower Heights Offensive*. Nors Swensen, a guard at the Company who remembers young Clayton very well, saw it last weekend. Said it gave him quite a turn. Showed the whole incident, the way Clayton saved his men and wiped out the Red machine-gun nest. I've been making inquiries to see whether it would be possible to rent the film to show here at the time of the Clayton festival."

"Was that when he was reported missing?" Leslie asked.

"Yes. He was never seen again."

Her father went out of the room and in a few minutes his shabby old Chevrolet, of which Agatha disapproved so vehemently—after all, he could have a Cadillac if he wanted it, nothing would give her more pleasure, and he really owed it to his position—drove around the house and turned toward the winding road along the river.

Rosie, the second maid, came into the breakfast room. Her eyes were like blue glassies and her cheeks like withered winter apples.

"It's Mr. Logan on the phone for you."

Leslie nodded. "Please excuse me, Aunt Agatha." In the library she picked up the telephone. "Hello, Paul."

"Hi, Beautiful," said a cheerful voice. "How about some tennis?"

"Oh, I'm sorry but not today. There's an errand I must do, so I'm going to New York."

There was an exaggerated sigh of disappointment and she laughed.

"Hardhearted Hannah," Paul Logan grumbled. "Why couldn't I have fallen for a more sympathetic girl?"

"Never mind," she mocked him, "Maybe the next one will be more satisfactory."

"Next one, indeed," he said indignantly, "when you can see me wasting away, day by day. I may be magnanimous enough to forgive you for that crack, but only if you promise to play golf at the club Saturday afternoon."

"Shylock! You and your pound of flesh," she said gaily.

"Will you?"

"I'd love it."

"Wonderful! Now don't let that local Lothario talk you out of it."

"I won't. And who is the local Lothario?"

"Oliver Harrison, of course. The Viking god. The Great Profile. As though you didn't know. But if I catch you swooning when he goes by——"

"You m-m-make me so m-m-mad," she sputtered.

He laughed. " 'By, Beautiful."

Leslie was laughing as she ran upstairs for gloves, handbag and car keys. When she came down, Agatha was crossing the wide hallway.

"Where are you going?"

Leslie counted slowly to ten and then said politely, "To see Jane Williams about the Douglas Clayton photographs."

"Will you be in for lunch?"

"I don't know. No, I won't. Whether Jane kept them or not, I think I'll run into New York and see that old documentary film. It might give me some ideas for the statue, some suggestions for action. I'll be home for dinner, in any case."

"Sometimes," Agatha said with an abruptness that was unlike her usual heavy placidity, "it seems to me that Douglas Clayton is more alive now than he ever was. He—he haunts this house!"

As though startled by her own vehemence, she added in her customary flat voice, "There's Hermann. Late as usual. I must speak to him about the flower beds. That spray he is using—" She went out on the lawn at her habitual firm, deliberate pace.

Leslie heard her say, "Hermann, I don't like—" She saw the controlled exasperation on the gardener's face. With a hopeless little shrug she went to the garage, backed out her small Renault, and wound down the windows. She took a long breath. It was a relief to escape from Agatha. For the hundredth time she wondered why on earth her father had married the woman.

*　　*　　*

Web Rock, the Williams house, was long, rambling and as modern as Telstar. Since the death of her husband, two years before, Jane Williams had lived there with her little son, Jack, and her young sister, Doris Brooke. Three indoor servants and a full-time gardener kept it in superb condition. From the time John Williams had built it for his bride, Web Rock had been the showplace of Claytonville.

The sisters were on the terrace at the back when Leslie arrived, discussing the best landscaping to set off the new swimming pool. Jack, tow-headed and freckled, who had seen the red Renault turn in at the driveway, raced to meet Leslie and tell her about it.

As she got out of the car he caught her arm, pulling her in his impatience. "C'mon, Leslie. Mom got an oval pool just to be different. Now she wants to put in some pink water lilies. Next thing we'll have swans. And I ask you, how can you swim with swans?"

The two sisters turned as Leslie came around the side of the house with Jack tugging at her hand. Leslie was struck, as always when she saw them together, by the difference between the sisters. It was not merely a matter of age, though Jane was ten years older than Doris. They were unlike in looks, in manner, in character. Jane was tall, misleadingly fragile in appearance, with blond hair, appealing blue eyes and a helpless manner. Doris was small and dark, with snapping black eyes and inexhaustible energy.

"Jack," his mother expostulated in her soft, rather fretful voice, "let Leslie alone! From the moment she enters this house you pester her."

"Well, gosh," he began. His hand tightened on Leslie's and she gave him a conspiratorial wink.

"Though I must say, Leslie," Jane went on, "you are partly to blame. Since he was knee-high you've spoiled him, telling him stories, playing with him. Now do run away, Jack, and don't make a nuisance of yourself."

He shuffled his feet. "Okay," he mumbled and wandered off, scuffing his shoes on the gravel of the driveway, head down in dejection.

"He's really fun, Jane," Leslie protested when he was out of hearing. "He doesn't bother me at all. And I love playing with him, you know. At that age, a child's imagination is so alive, so adventurous, that I find every minute I'm with him a delight. He's at the time of 'Let's pretend,' and there's no excitement like it in childhood."

"You ought to have him as a steady diet," Jane said. "You'd get as sick and tired of having him always underfoot as I do. He's reached the age when he never stops asking impossible questions: What makes the wind blow? How can we see things that are bigger than our eyes? Why are goldfish gold? Why? Why? Why? It's enough to drive any woman out of her mind."

Leslie bit back the words that crowded to her lips. She wondered how much love Jane could have had for her husband if she found their only child a nuisance. Perhaps, for once, Agatha Blake had been right when she said Jane had married John Williams simply because he was the richest available bachelor after Douglas Clayton died.

"Let's have some coffee," Jane suggested.

"I really can't stay," Leslie told her. "I'm going into New York to see that old war documentary about Douglas Clayton. I just stopped by here because I want to try to do a statue for the festival and I wondered if you still have any pictures of him. I haven't the slightest idea what he looked like."

"Good heavens, Leslie, that was years ago," Jane said in her plaintive voice. "I haven't the faintest memory of what I did with them. Probably they are stuck away in an old trunk somewhere. After he died and I met Jack, I naturally got rid of them. No man wants to look at the pictures of a younger and handsomer predecessor."

"Would it be an awful job to look for them?"

"Yes, it would," Jane said frankly. "Anyhow, there is something about going back, stirring up the past—well, it's hardly fair to ask that of me. Now is it?"

"No, I suppose it isn't," Leslie agreed. She flushed with embarrassment. "I just didn't realize how you felt about him."

"You were too young to remember Doug, or you would understand."

"We're the same age," Doris exclaimed, "and I remember him just as clearly as anything."

"But I never saw him at all," Leslie pointed out. "I never saw him in my life. We didn't come to Claytonville until after he died."

"Yes, of course," Jane said. "That was when your father inherited everything. I always knew Doug had a strong feeling of obligation about the Clayton Textile Company but, I must say, it was the biggest shock of my life when he left everything to your father, a distant cousin about five times removed, whom no one had ever heard of, just to keep it in the family, and didn't leave a thing to me. We'd been engaged a whole month before he went overseas, too, and he had had plenty of time to change his will. Naturally," she added, "I kept his diamond, but after I married Jack I wore it on my right hand."

She lifted her slender hand and the diamond blazed with light.

"What was he like?" Leslie asked.

"Heavens," Jane said with a reproachful look, "sometimes I think you have no real feelings at all, Leslie. He was the only man I ever really loved. Now let's—suppose we don't talk about him any more."

"I'm—honestly, I'm sorrier than I can say." Leslie put out her hand, pleading forgiveness, but Jane had turned away. Leslie gathered up her gloves and handbag.

"Wait, Leslie," Doris said eagerly, "let me go into New York with you. Do you mind?"

"I'd love it."

Several hours later, the girls were lunching at the Colony. Ever since the Blakes had moved to Claytonville, Doris Brooke, known as the Babbling Brooke to her friends, had been the closest thing to a sister that Leslie had ever known. As usual, Doris was chattering volubly, her black eyes snapping, cheeks flushed like a wild rose.

"So," she concluded, "Jane was shattered when Doug died. He was—well, he was absolutely wonderful: good-looking, gay, brilliant, sweet-tempered. He hated rows. I can still remember when people lost their tempers or got overheated in an argument, the way he would stop it by making such a ridiculous comment that the argument dissolved in laughter.

"Then the war. And the worst of it was that he didn't even have to go. He could have got out of it but he said he didn't particularly like the idea of someone doing his fighting for him and taking his risks while he sat it out in comfort at home.

"Three months after he reached Korea he wiped out that machine-gun nest. When word came that he was missing, presumed dead, Jane was stunned. She went around for weeks like a zombie. Then, about six months later, she married Jack. Of course, he was a lot older than she was but at least he didn't have to go off somewhere to fight."

"Only six months!" Leslie said in surprise.

"Well," Doris said practically, "Doug was gone and Jack wasn't the kind to wait around for her to make up her mind. Jane knew she'd never get another offer like that so she accepted him while she had the chance."

Leslie reached for the check in silence.

"Don't be too hard on Jane," Doris said unexpectedly. "You can stand on your own feet but she can't stand on hers. She needs someone to lean on, someone to take care of her. And, in a way, it was probably better all around that things happened as they did."

"Better?" Leslie was aware of a strong feeling of partisanship for the man who had not been remembered for six months.

"Well," Doris said, "I've often thought, suppose Doug had come back and he had been maimed in some way or disfigured. Jane has a—a kind of horror, a feeling of revulsion for anything like that. It really makes her ill. It would have been awful for both of them."

"But if she loved him—" Leslie began.

"There are all kinds of love," Doris said with unexpected shrewdness.

While they strolled along the Avenue she said, "Speaking of all kinds of love, how long are you going to keep Paul Logan dangling?"

Leslie laughed. "But I'm not!"

Doris hesitated, the color deepening in her cheeks. "Look, Leslie, you're so lovely you can get anyone you want. You always have a whole string of men. Are you serious about Paul?"

"No one could be serious about Paul. He's not serious about himself." Leslie thought of the gay, debonair young bachelor who was her shadow every minute that she allowed. "He's fun to be with," she said. "Lots of fun. Light-hearted and gay."

"But?" Doris probed with dogged persistence.

"But—that's all," Leslie said slowly. "I mean that he's satisfied just to play."

"Why not? He can afford it," Doris pointed out. "Look, Leslie, darling Leslie, if you don't want Paul, how about letting me have him? At least, you've got the glamorous Harrison man at your beck and call. Will you?" She broke off. "Oh, here's the theater. Let me get the tickets. You paid for lunch."

*   *   *

When the lights came on in the theater, the two girls got slowly to their feet, not yet ready to be jolted back into everyday life. Doris's eyelashes sparkled with tears.

"I didn't know it had been like that. Did you?" she asked huskily.

"I didn't know *he* had been like that," Leslie said softly. She was in a daze. While she walked beside Doris, a part of her still strained up a hill, through dust and machine-gun fire, accompanying the man who had clawed his way to meet the enemy single-handed. What had happened over the crest of the hill? How had Douglas Clayton met his lonely death? How had he felt as he hoisted himself over the top to face the enemy, single-handed and defenseless?

Doris had shaken off her emotion and was exclaiming about a cranberry-red evening dress in a shop window. If Paul saw her in that she'd make an impression he would never forget. She was still talking about it as they went down the stairs to the big rotunda in Grand Central Station. She looked at the big clock in dismay.

"Darn! We've missed the train. We'll have to wait for ages and ages. Jeepers!" She stopped short, staring at the tall man who had paused abruptly before her, who was running the fingers of his left hand through his hair. She clutched at Leslie's arm.

"Les!" she whispered. "That's exactly the way Doug moved and looked. It's Doug's gesture. I'd know it anywhere. Les! Do you suppose—"

Leslie shook off her hand, ran to touch the man's arm, her heart singing with gladness. "Douglas Clayton!" she cried out.

He wheeled around and she looked up, a long way up, into the grim face of a stranger.

Her hand dropped to her side. "Sorry," she said through dry lips. "My mistake."

As she turned back to Doris, the latter giggled nervously. "I guess we were both hypnotized by that movie. But what made you—I mean, after all, you never knew him—what made you seem so glad?"

"I don't know."

Doris looked at her friend in surprise, started to speak, and then, for once, the Babbling Brooke was silenced. She gave a quick glance over her shoulder. The stranger was still looking after them.

THE Clayton Textile Company sprawled over a number of acres of ground across the river from the village of Claytonville. It was much bigger than Donald Shaw had anticipated. The original building was now used for executive offices, and other buildings had been added—a laboratory for experimental chemists, and the big shops where the products were being manufactured.

The only approach from the village was through an old covered bridge that the people of Claytonville stubbornly refused to supersede by a more modern structure. Because he could not afford a car, Shaw had purchased a motorcycle of ancient vintage and equipped with a sidecar. It sounded like a freight train as it rumbled over the worn, uneven floor boards of the covered bridge.

In front of the main building the ground had been attractively landscaped, with well-cared-for lawns and varicolored flower beds. At one side a large parking area was marked off. Judging by the space allotted for employees' cars, the Clayton Company, he reflected, must support a vast majority of the people of the vicinity.

The spacious reception room was brightly lighted and impressive with its handsome draperies at the long windows, deep-piled carpet, and comfortable chairs with small tables. A first-rate decorator had obviously been at work to produce the results.

The receptionist was a pleasant young woman who welcomed him with a smile. He handed her his card.

"I have an appointment with Mr. Corliss Blake," he said.

She spoke over the telephone and then conducted him down a hallway to a corner office. It was large, comfortable and efficient, but there was no indication here that the president of the company had called upon the decorator's art. The desk was a battered old rolltop and the black leather chairs had seen many years of service.

On the desk there was a large framed photograph of a lovely girl with short copper curls, big brown eyes, a warm mouth and a chin whose firmness was softened by an unexpected dimple. Donald Shaw recognized the girl who had hailed him the day before in Grand Central Station with a gladness in her voice that still left him shaken when he thought of it. Hailed him as Douglas Clayton.

"That is my daughter," Corliss Blake said rather dryly, and with an effort Shaw pulled his eyes away from the smiling girl in the photograph to meet the unsmiling scrutiny of the man who had risen to greet him.

"She is very—lovely," he said quietly.

"Sit down, Mr. Shaw." Blake waved him to a chair. There was a thin folder lying before him, bearing the words *Donald Shaw*. "I am sorry there has been so long a delay about your application here. Your qualifications seem to be just what we want but there are other experimental chemists whose qualifications are equally good. Two others, as a matter of fact. I talked with them yesterday."

The eyes under the shaggy overhanging brows continued to study the younger man intently. Shaw felt his first qualm of uneasiness but he managed to remain relaxed and quiet in his chair, meeting those x-ray eyes, his own level.

"What we need here at this time," Blake told him abruptly, "goes beyond technical and scientific ability. We need a loyalty that is absolutely incorruptible. We're on the track of a new textile; there's no secret about that for the simple reason that there can't be. Rumors were flying months ago. That means the competition won't overlook anything to find out exactly what we are doing here."

"Particularly the Gypton Company," Shaw said in his deep, pleasant voice.

"You know them?"

"By reputation. Who doesn't?" Shaw smiled and his cold gray eyes warmed for a moment. "They dominate the field but they are as ruthless as gangsters from what I hear."

"And not above gangster methods, by all accounts." Blake pushed back his chair. "Would you like to look around the plant?"

Shaw was surprised but he answered promptly, "Very much."

By the end of an hour and a half, Shaw found himself lagging a trifle behind the older man. In a misleadingly casual manner, Corliss Blake had probed into his life, his opinions, his point of view on a dozen apparently unrelated topics that had no bearing on textiles. Little details that added up to a complete picture of a man. Keenly aware of what was happening, Shaw was careful to weigh every word he spoke, alert for the meanings that lay behind apparently innocent questions. He was keyed up, cautious, and beginning to tire physically.

Blake, who had been standing at a window, his back to Shaw, pointing out the site of the picnic grounds that were being laid out for the benefit of the employees, spoke gruffly, without turning around.

"You're exhausted. You should have told me. Suppose we go to lunch. We have a good restaurant here for our people. Run it at cost so that they get excellent food much more cheaply than they could elsewhere."

"I'd like that very much."

The eyes under the shaggy brows surveyed Shaw. "Been ill, haven't you?"

"Yes. I'm all right now though."

"Haven't got back your strength yet," Blake commented.

"I'm no invalid," Shaw declared. "I'm practically back to par. My physician has thrown me out because I'm much to healthy to bother with."

"Well," Blake said as he led the way to the restaurant on the top floor of the main building, "you'd probably better not try to do too much for the first few weeks. Work into it slowly."

It was a moment before Shaw grasped his meaning. "Does that—are you saying that I am hired?"

For the first time Corliss Blake smiled and Shaw saw a resemblance to his enchanting daughter. "Oh, yes, you're hired."

At a small table beside a window he seemed to become absorbed in the menu, giving his new employee time to recover his self-possession. Then he looked across the room and raised a finger. In a few minutes a man stood beside him, a tall, good-looking, blond man.

"Join us, won't you, Oliver?" Blake said.

"Delighted." The blond man pulled out a chair, looked curiously at Shaw.

"You must know each other," Blake said. "Mr. Oliver Harrison, our head chemist; Mr. Donald Shaw, our most recently acquired chemist."

Harrison's lips tightened for a moment with a shock of anger and then he held out his hand, trying to cover his fury. "Welcome to my department, Shaw. I'm sure we'll be able to work together."

There was a slight stress on the word "my." He was making clear that the head of the department was putting his subordinate in his place, and that the place was a minor one.

"It should be most interesting," Shaw said noncommittally.

"It occurred to me, Oliver," Blake said, "that you might be able to help Shaw find a suitable and comfortable place to live. I suppose," he added, looking at his new chemist, "you're at the Fox and Rabbit. Only inn we have within twenty-five miles. Of course, there are a couple of motels but—"

"Yes, I checked in at the Fox and Rabbit."

"Perhaps," Harrison said smoothly, "it might be as well to stay there for the present. You wouldn't want to commit yourself to a long-term lease until we know for sure whether or not you will be with us on a permanent basis."

Blake shot his head chemist a swift look and then devoted himself to his lunch. Donald Shaw, pouring dressing on his salad, was alerted to something odd in the situation. He had a curious feeling that Oliver Harrison held the whip hand over Corliss Blake. He looked up and met Harrison's eyes, read the naked hostility in them. A thrill ran along his nerves. Harrison was determined that Donald Shaw's term of employment with the Clayton Textile Company would be a brief one.

He returned the look. "You know," he said cheerfully, "I think I'm going to enjoy it here." He grinned.

Once more, Corliss Blake looked up swiftly, his eyes moving from face to face. Once more, he concentrated on his lunch, without speaking.

*   *   *

Next morning, Corliss Blake was standing on a ladder, pruning a tree, while his wife, as usual, gave directions and instructions.

Leslie ran across the lawn. "I'll be out for lunch, Aunt Agatha. All afternoon, in fact. Later, I'll be playing golf at the Country Club with Paul Logan."

She remembered Doris's pleading words and wondered what she could do about it: "I want someone who is always around to play with and Paul is lots of fun. I don't know what you expect of men, Leslie, but Paul's exactly my kind."

"Are you having lunch with Paul, too?" Agatha Blake asked.

"No, with Oliver Harrison. He just telephoned and, I don't know why, but he's a hard man to say 'no' to."

"I must say," Agatha remarked, "I don't know why you should say 'no' to Oliver. There's a lot more substance to a man like that than to an inveterate playboy like Paul Logan."

Sometimes, Leslie thought, Agatha revealed an unexpected amount of insight. She was right about Paul and Oliver.

"Playboy or not," Corliss said, "there's something very pleasant and trustworthy about Paul. I've always liked the boy."

"Oh, by the way, Corliss," Agatha asked, "did Oliver find you a new chemist?"

"No," Blake answered oddly, "I found my own. I selected the man I thought would fill the bill. Matter of fact," there was a glint in his eyes, "I suspect that he'll quite possibly do rather better than that."

Agatha sighed. "I must say, in a matter of this kind, where the requirements are so specialized, Oliver would know best."

There was a look of amusement on Blake's face. "I rather imagine that Oliver would agree with you."

"Well, then?"

"You may both be right, my dear," he said pacifically. "Time will tell. And yet it has been my observation all my life that a man's achievements rest less on his abilities than they do on his character. It's not what a man can do; it's what he will do. That's why you find so many brilliant failures, so many people of no more than average talent who succeed. They have put to use all they had while the other fellow either misused or misdirected it."

He climbed down from the ladder and smiled at his daughter. "You're looking very bonnie in that pale yellow dress. As crisp and fragrant and sweet as a daffodil. Like spring walking."

"Dad! How lovely of you."

"Is that in Oliver's honor?" There was something searching in the look Blake gave his daughter.

Leslie felt the warm color washing over her face. She couldn't say that two days earlier she had looked for a startled moment at a strange man and suddenly she had known the meaning of spring magic.

"It's—I just felt spring in the air, I guess."

"You're like your mother." As her father spoke, Leslie caught her breath in surprise. It was the first time he had ever referred to his first wife in Agatha's presence. "She was always infected with spring madness; I used to tell her that she was never responsible for what she did in the spring."

Agatha's full mouth was rather pinched. She turned away to look fixedly at the tree which he had been pruning.

A big white Chrysler came purring up the driveway. Oliver Harrison got out and strolled over to greet them, his blond hair shining like a Viking's under the sun, good-looking face alight. For a moment he paused, turned to look at a flower bed, presenting what Paul Logan had called "The Great Profile."

Leslie found herself struggling not to laugh. You couldn't laugh at Oliver. Oliver never laughed at himself. She remembered now, early in their acquaintance, she had said that people needed laughter, particularly needed to laugh at themselves, in order to keep their perspective, not to take themselves too seriously; above all, not to be bogged down in self-pity.

Oliver had taken a firm stand. He disagreed entirely. "If a man laughs at himself," he had pointed out in dead seriousness, "there is always a chance that other people will laugh at him. And laughter can be fatal, the most fatal weapon there is. No, it doesn't pay for a man to laugh at himself."

As usual, Oliver turned first to Agatha who expanded with pleasure at his attentive manner, his fulsome compliments. Then he spoke to Corliss Blake in a tone that, for all its courtesy, held an undercurrent of condescension.

"Morning, Mr. Blake. I'm borrowing your lovely daughter for a while."

"Quite all right, Oliver. Home for dinner, dear?"

"Six-thirty at the latest," Leslie promised and let Oliver help her into the car. He did things like that gracefully but with a manner that reminded her irresistibly of Sir Walter Raleigh spreading his cloak for Queen Elizabeth. Something had gone wrong for her today. She must stop seeing everything as either incredibly wonderful or incredibly absurd.

"Heavens," she exlaimed, "what luxury! You must be trying to impress me."

Oliver slid under the wheel, his manner a trifle stuffy, and she recalled with compunction that he mustn't be teased either.

"I wish I could impress you," he said soberly as he turned the car and headed for the center of the village.

"This is new, isn't it?"

He smiled with a flash of white teeth. "A custom-made job. I ordered it some time ago. It was just delivered this morning. That's why I was so insistent about lunch. You simply had to be the first person to ride in it."

Something in his tone bothered her. He was, she thought, assuming too much. She didn't know how to answer him.

If she displayed too much pleasure in the car, or if she hurt him by ignoring his tacit assumption of her right to an interest in it, she would be wrong either way.

She compromised by leaning forward to look at the dashboard and to ask for an explanation of all the gadgets. Oliver beamed and explained everything in detail, talking, as he always did to women, as though they needed to be addressed in the simplest terms in order to understand anything.

He pulled up behind the Claytonville taxi, irritated at having his dashing approach to the inn spoiled. Under the machine-gun fire from the eyes of the rocking chair brigade on the porch, a young woman stepped out of the taxi, a supersmart redhead, in a beautifully cut black linen dress. While the taxi driver helped the doorman to carry in half a dozen assorted suitcases and hatboxes, she stared down the eyes that watched her; then she turned with a graceful, insolent movement and caught sight of the white Chrysler. Her green eyes under slanting brows, carefully darkened, moved from the car to the blond man at the wheel, traveled on to Leslie. She turned her back on them and strolled into the inn.

"Well," Leslie exclaimed, "I wonder who the redheaded siren is?"

"Never saw her in my life," Oliver answered. He pulled up with a flourish under the big, brilliantly painted sign that showed a red fox in pursuit of a rabbit with shell-pink ears.

The doorman hurried out. "Yes, sir."

"Park it for me," Oliver said curtly and followed Leslie into the dining room.

"Afternoon, Miss Blake. Afternoon, sir."

The "sir" made Oliver compress his lips. The headwaiter always made a point of addressing his more distinguished patrons by their names. Apparently, even after nine months in Claytonville, Oliver was still regarded as an outsider; or, intolerable supposition, as not sufficiently distinguished to rate the headwaiter's seal of approval.

The headwaiter gave them a choice window table that looked out on a small pond behind the inn with weeping willows around its rim. The willows had already changed from their spring yellow to a delicate green.

"Another few days like this, Miss Blake, and we'll be serving out on the lawn. Mark my words."

When they had ordered, Leslie half expected Oliver to force the conversation into personal channels, as he had been increasingly inclined to do during the past month. Instead, he was unusually silent, plunged into thoughts that, to judge by his expression, were unpleasant. She realized that he was forcing himself to respond to her light chatter about golf and the coming tennis championship matches and Jane Williams's new swimming pool at Web Rock.

"It sounds like a gay season," he said as she came to the end of her light-hearted comments.

"Yes," she agreed, "only—"

"Only—what?" He had put aside, for the time being, the troublesome problem he had been dealing with. He gave her the warm intimate smile that had made half the girls in Claytonville fall in love with him and had won the enthusiastic support of all the older women.

"Only I don't want to spend the summer just playing," she admitted. "I'd like to do something that, well, that mattered at least a little bit."

"Such as?"

"For one thing, I'm going back to sculpting. I haven't touched it for nearly a year."

He paid the check, ostentatiously added too large a tip, and pulled back her chair before the waiter could reach it. He took her arm as they went through the lobby and out to the waiting Chrysler. There was an intangible air of proprietorship in his manner.

The doorman said, "Sir, that's a brand-new car but I noticed, though there's only a few miles on it—"

Oliver stared him down and got back under the wheel. Leslie was reminded irresistibly of the Shakespeare character: "And when I ope my lips, let no dog bark."

"You still have an hour before your date with Logan. Shall we take a little run and try it out?"

"As long as we get back in time. I don't like to be late for appointments."

"Promptness is the courtesy of kings," he quoted. "Is that what you mean?" Before she could speak he added resentfully, "There is something about the Clayton name and everyone associated with it; they all develop the kingly manner."

"That's just plain silly, Oliver!" Leslie protested angrily.

"Is it?" For a moment his face had a sullen cast. Then he smiled at her. "My mistake."

They left the village behind and Oliver chose a winding, tree-lined road along which the car purred smoothly.

"Leslie," he said without warning, "I'm in love with you, and I want you to marry me. You're everything I want in a wife, beautiful and sweet and charming. Everything I want. Dignity and breeding. More than I," there was a fractional pause, "than I ever expected to find. And I could make you happy. I know I could."

"Oh, Oliver," she exclaimed in distress, "I'm so sorry. I didn't mean this to happen."

There was amusement in his good-looking face. "I did."

"I—I like you enormously." (That's not really true, she thought; I feel uneasy when I'm with you.) "But I couldn't marry you. I'm not in love with you."

To her surprise he gave her a confident smile. "Honey, you don't know anything about it. I've looked over my competition here, of course. With the exception of Paul Logan, there's no man near your own age who could interest you in the least. A run-of-the-mill lot. You deserve something better."

Leslie struggled not to laugh. Of all the conceit!

He went on with smooth assurance, "I'll teach you to love me. We'll have a good life."

"What do you mean, a good life?"

"What everyone means," he said, a touch of impatience in his voice. Then he smiled confidently again. "There's no reason why I shouldn't eventually be top man in the Company. I've got what it takes, more than—" He stopped, then went on more carefully "I've thought of buying that parcel of land that lies beyond your father's house and building on it. Something, perhaps, along the lines of Web Rock. A real attention-getter. Then, some day, we'll be able to combine the two properties and have a really impressive estate."

"You've thought it all out, haven't you?"

He did not hear the warning in her voice. "Of course I have. No man can build a career haphazardly. He plans it, step by step."

"Including his wife?" Leslie asked with dangerous demureness.

"Including—" He checked himself abruptly. Then he stopped the car, reached for her. "Leslie, my darling."

She held him away from her, her hands pressing hard against his chest. "No, Oliver! Please don't."

He laughed, tried to draw her close to him in spite of her resistance. His eyes fell on the dashboard. He straightened up with a start, releasing her.

"The good-for-nothing—that jerk at the garage—I'll have his job for this!"

Staggered by the sudden change in his voice, Leslie stammered, "Wh-what's wrong?"

"Look at that gauge! In the red. A brand-new car and they didn't even service it properly. No oil! No telling what harm has been done to the motor!"

He saw her expression of distaste and tried to conceal his rage, since he could not control it. He drew a long breath, forced a laugh, and managed to say more calmly, "Well, here we sit until we can get help. I won't take a chance on driving as much as one more foot." He slipped an arm around her. "Let's look at the bright side. I've got you to myself. I'm going to prove that you—like me—more than you think you do." He repeated triumphantly, "I've got you." His arms tightened.

A noisy motorcycle came around the curve and Oliver touched his horn. "Hey, there," he shouted, waving his hand.

The motorcycle slowed. Stopped. The rider pushed up his goggles and Leslie looked into deep-set gray eyes. She groped for the handle of the door, almost unconsciously, her heart like a songbird launching itself on the air.

"Need any help?" said a deep, pleasant voice. "Oh, it's you, Harrison."

"Hello, Shaw. Yes, I need help. The da—the stupid fool who delivered this car didn't put in any oil. Call the Standard Company and tell them to send a tow truck. This car isn't going a single foot until the motor has been checked. Oh, and send the taxi out for us."

The easy, arrogant authority with which he issued his orders, the dictatorial voice, brought soft color to the girl's face and defiant sparks to her eyes. She opened the door and got out.

"Where are you going?" Harrison demanded.

"I have an engagement at the Country Club," she reminded him, the words stumbling over each other in her haste, "and I'll be terribly late if I wait for the taxi. It's probably meeting the afternoon train now and may take another hour before it can get here."

"I want to talk to you." Harrison leaned across the seat but Leslie had already closed the door.

She looked at the stranger on the motorcycle. "Do you suppose—could you take me—at least partway—to the Country Club in your sidecar?"

"Of course. Hop in."

Shaw waited until the girl was seated and then flipped his hand casually at the blond man who smoldered behind the wheel of the motionless white car. It might have been merely a gesture of farewell but there was an undercurrent of mockery. In a series of noisy explosions the motorcycle moved off.

iv

SITTING in the sidecar, Leslie looked up shyly at the driver.
With the heavy goggles covering his eyes again there was
only the firm chin, the mouth with its bitter lines, to show
what manner of man he was. Oliver had known him but
he must be a stranger in Claytonville. In a village of that
size it was impossible that she would not have noticed him
before.

Leslie was so intent on the silent man, so absorbed, that
she paid no attention to the road beyond being aware that
the man whom Oliver had called Shaw was going very
slowly. Then he gave a sharp exclamation as he caught
sight of four deer preparing to leap a fence onto the road,
and the motorcycle rocketed around a corner of the dusty
highway with a speed which sent the sidecar into the air
and draped the passenger over the driver's shoulder.

He slowed, stopped. She clung to him, her soft cheek
pressed against his hair. Gently he released her, settled her
in the sidecar. His face was dead white.

"Are you all right?"

"Yes," she said with an odd breathlessness.

"That was inexcusable of me. I'm not used to this thing
yet. I didn't realize it would—are you sure you aren't hurt?"

She smiled at him. "Perfectly sure."

"Still trust me to get you to the Country Club in one
piece?"

"I'll trust you," she said gravely.

"That's—more than I deserve. But thank you." The motorcycle moved off again. It was difficult to talk above the
noise of the motor. He laughed. "The signs mean something."
He stopped beside a gate with the sign: "Cattle crossing."
Across the road came a herd of cows headed toward the
milking barn, prodded by a barefoot boy of about twelve
in blue jeans and a red shirt, a broad straw hat on his

28

head. In the sudden quiet Leslie heard the rustling of leaves and the song of a bird.

"What a beautiful world," she said unsteadily, her eyes fixed on the glistening water of a pool whose blue reflected the sky. Now that he had removed the goggles she found it hard to look at him.

"Miss Blake," he began abruptly.

She looked at him then in surprise. "You know who I am?"

"I saw a photograph of you yesterday on your father's desk. I am Donald Shaw, a new chemist at the Company."

"Oh, of course. He was speaking of you this morning. I hope you'll like it here."

He turned to face her. "Tell me, Miss Blake, when we —met—in Grand Central Station the other day, did you mistake me for a friend of yours?"

She was aware of the blood that flushed her cheeks and pounded in her veins. "No, I mistook you for a man I have never seen in my life. A man named Douglas Clayton. This village was named for his great-great-grandfather. The textile company was his. He was the only one left of his family, except for my father who was a distant cousin. He died in Korea."

Her throat closed for a moment. Her eyelashes sparkled. She wiped away the tears. "He died gloriously to save his company. You must have heard of him. There was so much written about him by men whose lives he had saved by his sacrifice. Everything we have we owe to him because my father inherited his house, his business, his money, everything he had."

She was silent for a moment and the man watched the play of expression on her face. He did not make any comment.

"Well," she said, drawing a long breath, "a statue may be erected to him here in Claytonville, if I can do it well enough. I didn't know what he looked like, so I asked the girl he had been engaged to marry, but she said that if she still had any pictures of him they must be stuck away somewhere in an old trunk. I went into New York to see an army documentary film that showed the—the magnificent thing he did."

She was silent for a long time, living over that experience. Then the brown eyes lifted to his and she gave him a wavering smile.

"It certainly takes me long enough to get at the point," she said with an attempt at gaiety. "Anyhow, I went with

my best friend, Doris Brooke, whose sister was Douglas
Clayton's fiancée. She remembered him very clearly and we
were thinking of him, of course, and then, at the station,
the way you stood, the way you ran your fingers through
your hair, Doris said it was like Doug. And then—" Her
voice trailed off, her brown eyes stared insistently at a
forsythia bush as though she had never seen one before.
She did not look up.

"But you sounded—glad," Donald Shaw said. "Don't you
realize that if I really had been this fellow Clayton, you
and your father might be in an awkward position in regard
to the inheritance?"

The brown eyes blazed with sudden anger. "Do you think,"
she sputtered, "for one single moment we'd rather have that
than have him safely home?"

Steady gray eyes looked deep into indignant brown ones,
warmed, and a smile transformed his face. It was like—like
a candle being lighted in her heart. What's happened to me,
she wondered in alarm. I don't know this man. There is
something about him, the grimness, the bitterness in his
face, that means something terrible has happened to him.
And yet—

Shaw glanced at his watch. "I'm making you late for
your appointment, as well as delaying Harrison. He won't
like that."

"You'll be in the same department, won't you?"

"In *his* department, as I understand it. Great friend of
yours?"

The comment was casual but Leslie was aware that Shaw
must have seen Oliver's arms around her, her hands holding
him off. "The people who work for the firm are all very
friendly," she said, "and Mr. Harrison seems to be quite
popular. He has gone ahead unusually fast."

"A man on his way," Shaw commented without any in-
flection in his voice.

"That's what my father feels. And especially my stepmother."

"If he can maintain a car like that, he's doing all right."

"Oh, he has some money of his own, I believe." Leslie
hesitated. "If you are going to work together, you ought
to have an opportunity to be better acquainted. Every Sunday
evening at seven we give a buffet supper for people from
the Company. Won't you join us tomorrow evening, Mr.
Shaw?"

"Thank you. With great pleasure." The last of the cattle
had crossed the road and the motorcycle roared off. Neither
of them attempted to speak again until he had turned into

the driveway leading to the Country Club. Before he could dismount to help her, Paul Logan came running down the steps from the veranda.

"Leslie! I've been worried. What happened? An accident?"

"Paul, I want you and Mr. Shaw to know each other. Paul Logan. Mr. Shaw has joined the Company as an experimental chemist."

The two men shook hands, the slim man with the light brown hair, a pleasant face and cheerful smile, with something incurably boyish about it. As usual he was smoothly turned out, in contrast to the older man, who was casually dressed in shabby slacks and pullover, and whose face would be strikingly handsome if it were not so stern.

"Mr. Shaw," Leslie went on, the dimple flashing, "has just rescued me."

"Accident?" Paul repeated sharply.

"No." In spite of herself, Leslie gave a soft gurgle of laughter. "It's a shame to laugh but it was funny. Oliver Harrison has a brand-new Chrysler, custom-made, and he is so proud of it. But the garage forgot to put in any oil before it was delivered."

"You break my heart," Paul said with great pleasure. "I'd love to see Harrison the Great sitting behind the wheel of a car that can't run. In fact, I wouldn't mind seeing him under the wheels of a car that could."

"Paul!"

"Mark my words, Beautiful, that guy is so slick he's bound to skid one of these days and I only hope I'll be there to see it. Thanks a lot, Shaw, for lifesaving my gal for me." He caught her hand. "Come on. I give you exactly two minutes to change those shoes."

They ran laughing toward the clubhouse. At the door Leslie paused to turn and wave. Shaw lifted his hand in salute and the motorcycle roared back to the road.

*   *   *

Leslie and Paul sat at one of the small tables on the lawn under a huge, brightly colored umbrella. They were both flushed and laughing. The waiter set tall, frosted glasses before them, gin and tonic for Paul, plain tonic for Leslie.

"I think you do it on purpose," he accused her.

"Do what?"

"Keep me laughing. To throw me off my game. You can't make me believe you won honestly."

She made a face at him. "Poor loser," she jeered.

His expression changed. He leaned across the table, covered one of her slim hands with his broader one.

"Beautiful, let's get married this summer. I'm crazy about you. There's no one I have more fun with. Say yes, Sweetie. We'd have a good life, together. A swell life."

That was what Oliver had said. A good life.

"What do you mean—a good life?" she asked.

"One wonderful day after another," he said eagerly. "I'm not a rich man, just the thirty thousand a year my aunt left me. But think what we could crowd into our lives: travel, cruises, Florida in winter or the Riviera or even those African safaris that are supposed to give people status. If that matters. Dancing, bridge, swimming, golf, tennis, sailing. All the year round. A holiday three hundred and sixty-five days a year. And you, lovely and sweet and gay, to share all the laughs."

He added more seriously, "All your beauty and sweetness. More than I deserve, I know; more than any man deserves."

She left her hand in his and smiled while she shook her head.

"Why not? Don't you like me at all?"

"More than that. I'm very fond of you. But—"

"But?"

"I'm the wrong girl for you, Paul dear. You are tuning in on the wrong wavelength. I'm much too—sobersides for you. I couldn't live a life that was all vacation. I like fun, but not all the time, not just fun as a goal. It would never satisfy me, so I would never satisfy you."

She drew her hand away gently. "You need a girl like —well, like Doris Brooke. She could give you what you are looking for and you—"

"Doris? The Babbling Brooke? Why, compared with you—"

"Wait, Paul," Leslie said hastily, "don't say anything unkind about Doris."

"I wasn't going to be unkind. She's cute as a button and lots of fun. For my money she's twice as attractive as Jane, for all Jane's beauty. But—"

"She likes you, Paul," Leslie said softly. "She likes you very, very much."

"Oh," he said rather blankly. He scribbled his name on the check, summoned up a teasing smile. "Shall I take you home, Sobersides?"

When she had showered and changed for dinner, Leslie went down to the library where she found her father and stepmother. The latter, busy with some lists she was making, was quiet for once.

Blake put down his evening paper and smiled. "Had a nice day?"

"Very." Leslie had no intention of telling Agatha about her two proposals. The dimple flashed.

"What's the joke?" her father asked.

She told him about Oliver Harrison's trouble with the new car and how Donald Shaw had come to the rescue on a beaten-up old motorcycle.

"He told me he was your new chemist," she said.

Her father nodded thoughtfully. "He struck me as the right man for the job. Straight as a die, or I'm no judge of men. He doesn't seem to be up to par physically. He tires very soon. I have the impression that he has gone through a long and serious illness, though he doesn't want to talk about it. He assured me he was all right. I have a hunch that Harrison is going to give him a rough time. He wasn't pleased by my choice."

Agatha looked up from her lists. "Well, I must say, Corliss, he can't be blamed for wanting to select his own men. And I'm dreadfully sorry about his new car. Dreadfully."

"I asked Mr. Shaw to come to the buffet supper tomorrow evening, Aunt Agatha."

"Dear me, I hope he's presentable."

"Entirely presentable," her husband assured her dryly. "In fact, I'd say he is an exceptionally distinguished-looking man."

"Oh, and I asked Paul Logan, too."

"But he's not in the Company, Leslie," her stepmother protested, "and we have always restricted the Sunday night parties to the personnel."

"I know, Aunt Agatha. I only thought, if it's all right with you, I'd ask Doris to pour so I can circulate more among the guests. And with Paul to dance with she won't feel like the only outsider."

"If we're going to let down the bars," Agatha said in resignation, "you might as well ask Doris, if you want her. But in that case, you'll have to include her sister, too. It won't matter too much this time. With all the flu that is going around I've had several refusals."

She added names to her list. "A Miss Felice Allen telephoned this afternoon. She has a syndicated fashion column, covering highlights all over the country." In spite of herself, Agatha could not conceal her satisfaction. "She asked if she might come tomorrow evening to cover our little party, though I explained that it is quite an informal affair. I simply didn't know how to refuse. She is staying at the Fox and Rabbit for a few weeks of rest, but you know what these columnists are, always on the lookout for something that's newsworthy."

She looked at Leslie, frowning. "I do wish she had given me more warning, though. You should have a new dress as long as Miss Allen is a fashion expert."

"I'll wear the green one."

"But you wore that two weeks ago."

"She won't know that," Leslie said cheerfully, "and I can't see that it really matters."

"My dear, even if you don't care about Miss Allen's opinion, haven't you noticed that Oliver Harrison has a real eye for women's clothes?"

"Then he can look at you in that new black dress," Leslie said. "That ought to be enough for anyone."

For a fleeting moment there was the suggestion of a simper on Agatha's face. "It was extravagant of me, but I always feel that it pays to buy the best clothes. And, after all, I got it with my own money."

If just one whole day could pass, Leslie thought, later that night, as she sat before her mirror in white crepe pajamas, brushing her short curls, just one single day when Aunt Agatha didn't refer to "my own money." Just one.

She put down her brush, pulled a negligee over her shoulders, switched off the lights and went to stand at the window, looking out at the familiar landscape that, bathed in moonlight, became strange, a dream-world.

Moonlight had always seemed magical to her, and the moon itself a place of dreams. It was a pity that men were determined to wrest its last secrets from it, to make it as prosaic as Main Street, to invade its stillness with their noise, its unbroken peace with their unrest.

What a curious day it had been! Two men had asked her to marry them. Two good-looking, prosperous men, both of whom seemed to love her, each of whom had promised her "a good life."

What different meanings the most familiar words had for different people. Oliver wanted a successful career and prosperity and importance. She looked out on the land beyond the gardens, the land that Oliver intended to buy. To buy and, when her father was dead, combine with the Clayton property. And he had made clear that he had his eye on her father's job, too. Probably he was counting the years until his retirement or—or—

Standing in the dark, looking out on the milky world, the garden whose flowers were colorless under the moon, the slender girl found herself shaking not with cold but with sudden anger. She was simply a necessary part of a real estate deal. That was one element of his carefully planned career that Oliver Harrison would have to abandon.

She thought of him, raging and helpless, behind the wheels of the motionless car, and giggled.

A good life. Those had been Paul's words, too. Dear Paul, sweet and gay and easygoing. Paul for whom every day was a holiday. While Oliver had been amused by her rejection of his proposal, supremely confident that he could persuade her in the end, Paul had been genuinely hurt. He really cared about her. But when he thought it over, when he realized that she couldn't fit into his plans for a good life, he'd find a girl who could. And then he would be happy, happier than he could ever be with her.

Perhaps, she thought, troubled, she shouldn't have told him about Doris. No, it was the kind of shock treatment that would be bound to arouse his interest in her, make him notice her as a person. He would see for himself, eventually, that Doris was the right kind of girl for him, a girl who could "share all the laughs." And, because he lacked Oliver Harrison's inordinate and unscrupulous vanity, nothing in his manner would ever lead Doris to guess that he knew her secret.

Leslie dropped her negligee over a chair, slipped off her satin mules and got into bed. Two hours later she was still staring wide-eyed at the window. Perhaps it was the moonlight that kept her awake. Perhaps.

She saw deep-set gray eyes that had looked on horror, and a mouth that had experienced terrible things. A mouth that could smile unexpectedly, lighting a candle in her heart.

She turned restlessly, pressing her cheek against the smooth cool pillow. It was the moonlight that had made her sleepless. It couldn't be anything else.

He's coming here tomorrow evening, she thought. I'll be seeing him again. She smiled and fell asleep.

v

THERE were two institutions in Claytonville that were observed as regularly as the stars wheeling through the sky. One was Sunday brunch at the Fox and Rabbit, the other was the Sunday buffet supper given by the head of the Clayton Textile Company for his employees, entertaining them in rotation, about twenty at a time.

At eleven, on the following morning, Leslie sat at a table for four on the enclosed porch of the Fox and Rabbit, a compromise between the restaurant proper and the lawn, as the sky was cloudy and there was a chilly breeze. According to unalterable custom, too, folding tables beside each large table held bulky Sunday newspapers.

Leslie, buttering a popover, nodded and greeted friends at the other tables. Her own was the most silent. Doris was looking at the fashion section of the *New York Times* while her older sister was engrossed in a special article in the magazine section. Jack was giving all his attention to single-minded absorption in a waffle.

There was a slight stir, a murmur of comment, a whiff of perfume, and the redheaded girl who had arrived the day before followed the headwaiter to a small table against the wall. She walked like a model, erect and graceful, wearing a white linen suit of impeccable cut and a big black cartwheel hat. She frowned in annoyance and spoke sharply to the headwaiter, who indicated with a helpless gesture that all the window tables were occupied.

Doris looked up from the fashion page. "How stunning that black and white combination is with her red hair. She's really something. Makes me feel like a country mouse. I wonder who she is and what she's doing here. Not visiting anyone or she wouldn't be alone."

As though aware that she was being discussed, the redheaded girl looked across the porch at them. For a moment the long narrow green eyes examined them without blinking, like a cat's eyes, and then went coolly back to the big menu.

Doris flushed. "She certainly cut me down to size," she said ruefully. "Serves me right for staring at her."

"I think," Leslie told her, "that must be Miss Allen, who has a syndicated fashion column. She's staying here at the inn. Vacation or something."

"How on earth did you get the lowdown?" Doris asked.

"She called Aunt Agatha and said she'd like to cover the buffet supper tonight. Oh, and that reminds me—we hope you'll both come."

"I thought the buffet suppers were reserved exclusively for the Company."

"As a rule, yes. But tonight I thought perhaps you'd pour so I could circulate."

Doris laughed. "I might have known there would be a catch in it. But it would be fun. Of course, I'll pour."

"And you, Jane?"

Jane looked up from her paper. In a pale blue dress, her blond hair brushed smoothly back, her blue eyes wide and appealing, she was easily, Leslie thought, the loveliest woman in the room.

"Mother," Jack said urgently, "how's about another waffle?"

Jane signaled a waiter and then said vaguely, "Well, I don't know, Leslie. If that fashion expert is going to be there, it would be hard to compete." For Jane any other young woman automatically became competition.

"Not for you," Leslie assured her with so much genuine admiration that Jane smiled. She opened her handbag and fumbled for a mirror. A crumpled envelope fell out and an alert waiter retrieved it.

Jane looked at it, the smile fading. "Oh, dear, I've got to write to Mary and I simply don't know what to say. It's so terrible."

"Mary Williams? Your sister-in-law?" Leslie asked.

Jane nodded. "Of course, she's at least thirty-eight and I suppose she is willing to settle for anything just to get married but—oh, dear!"

"What's wrong with the man?" Doris asked.

"He's a war casualty," Jane explained. "He lost part of one leg, just below the knee. Mary says he has only the slightest limp but, good heavens, just imagine it! Why, they wouldn't even be able to dance together. And even if it isn't noticeable to other people, she'd always know that he was not completely right."

"But suppose she loves him," Leslie expostulated. "There

are so many worse things, things like cruelty and dishonesty, like cheating and exploiting people, like alcoholism and irresponsibility. I can't see that a small thing like that would matter in the least."

Jane shivered. "I'd rather never marry. Never. Never."

There was so much revulsion in her face that Leslie said quickly, "What have you been reading with so much interest?"

It was as easy to divert Jane's attention as it was a small baby's.

"My dear, the most extraordinary thing. All about fake heirs and the way some of them deceived people for years and years. One even convinced the mother of the real heir that he was her own son."

"That doesn't seem possible." Doris's face brightened and Leslie knew, without turning around, what had brought that sunny look to her friend's face.

"Hi, Paul," Doris called.

He looked around, smiled, waved his hand, and joined some friends at a distant table.

Doris's face fell, but Leslie understood how awkward it would be for Paul Logan to find himself at the same table with a girl he loved and another girl who loved him.

"You'll be seeing him tonight," she said quickly. "He's coming to the buffet supper."

"The trouble with you, Doris," Jane told her younger sister, "is that you show your hand. Be hard to get. Any woman who plays her cards right can have any man she wants, but she looks like a better bargain to him if she seems to be moving away instead of running after him."

Doris flushed hotly. For a moment she appeared almost sick with embarrassment.

"Mother," Jack asked, "can I have another waffle?"

"I suppose so, but I'm sure I don't know what you do with all that food."

"He's got a hollow leg," Leslie declared. "I've noticed it before. It floats when he's swimming. Helps to hold him up. Very convenient. Everyone should be equipped the same way."

Jack giggled. He found everything Leslie said riotously funny. "Leslie," he begged, "c'mon over and swim at our house as soon as we get through here."

"No swimming for you, young man," his mother said, "for at least two hours after the meal you've been putting away."

"Soon," Leslie promised the disappointed small boy. "I'll come soon. But this afternoon I have to help Aunt Agatha with some arrangements for the party. Anyhow, it's much too chilly to swim yet. Wait until we've had a few hot days to warm up the water."

"Aw," Jack began. The waiter removed his plate and set another waffle in front of him. He reached for his butter knife and checked to make sure the syrup pitcher was near at hand.

Jane had been looking around the porch. "What this village needs is some new blood. Except for that redheaded vixen, there's not a new face in the place."

Doris laughed. Her exuberant vitality always amazed Leslie when she contrasted it with Jane's languor. "Why vixen?"

Jane shrugged. "Any woman who is smart evaluates the competition."

She sounds like Oliver Harrison, Leslie thought in surprise. Perhaps they would make a good combination. She checked her wayward thoughts with inner amusement. Good heavens, I'm turning into a marriage broker.

"That woman," Jane went on, "is like a fox. Look at her narrow pointed face and those strange green eyes. If I know anything about my own sex, she is a woman who is all set to pounce."

She broke off while the waiter refilled their cups with coffee and brought Jack another glass of milk. "By the way, what's this about a glamorous stranger in town? I was playing bridge with the Kelseys last night and Helen Kelsey said she had met him at the drugstore. Perry Kelsey introduced him. A newcomer at the Company."

To the people of Claytonville, the Clayton Textile Company was always the Company with a capital C.

"Helen said he was one of the most charming men she had ever met, and much the best-looking."

Leslie had never sounded so casual, so indifferent. "That must be the new chemist. His name is Donald Shaw. You'll meet him tonight."

"Now there's a new face for you, Jane!" Doris exclaimed.

Jane shook her head. "Not for me," she said with unac-customed firmness. "Helen said he went off on an old bat-tered-up motorcycle. And Perry told me he'd admitted that he couldn't afford to buy a car. Just laughed about it. A man like that probably couldn't even take a girl out to a decent dinner."

Doris's eyes, in spite of Jane's warning, had continued to travel wistfully to the table where Paul Logan was sitting. Like a needle to the north, Leslie thought. Paul waved his hand and called cheerfully, "Hey, Shaw! Join us, won't you?"

A tall man answered the wave, nodded, and strolled the length of the porch.

"Why," Doris exclaimed, "that—"

The man's casual glance fell on their table. He stopped abruptly, as though shocked. Then, as Leslie smiled a welcome, he came toward them.

Leslie held out her hand. "Good morning, Mr. Shaw. Let me introduce you to my friends, Mrs. Williams, Miss Brooke, and Jack Williams. Mr. Shaw."

Jane nodded. "How do you do?"

Doris said eagerly, "Why, you're the man in Grand Central Station!"

He smiled. "I am, indeed. But from now on I'm the man in Claytonville."

"I'm so glad," Doris said cordially.

Shaw shook hands gravely with the nine-year-old boy who had stood up when Leslie introduced them.

"Do you really have a motorcycle?" Jack asked.

"I really have."

"Can I ride on it sometime?"

"Jack!" his mother protested. She turned big blue eyes on the newcomer. "How on earth," she said plaintively, "do people ever succeed in teaching small boys manners? If you ask me, they're all just natural savages."

Jack sat down, his face flushed, and pushed away the rest of his waffle.

"Jane!" Doris said sharply. "Jane, is anything wrong?"

Jane's face was usually pale, but it was a healthy pallor. Now, however, it was dead white.

"Why should there be?" she asked petulantly.

Donald Shaw gave her a keen look and then leaned forward to hold a glass of water to her lips, steadying it for her. "Drink this."

She sipped it, set it down. "Silly of me. I'm quite all right now."

With another long look at her, Shaw bowed and went to join Paul and his friends. It was like Paul, Leslie thought gratefully, to try to make the stranger feel at home. The stranger who had paid no attention to her after he had seen Jane Williams's fragile loveliness.

"Let's go," Jane said, pushing her chair back before the waiter could reach her.

They followed her out to the sleek black Cadillac. Without protest, Jane let Doris take the wheel. Jack scrambled into the front seat beside his aunt and Leslie sat beside Jane in back. Jane slumped, resting her head against the back of the seat.

"Feel better?" Doris called over her shoulder as the car slid away from the curb.

"It wasn't anything really," Jane said. "Just a kind of

shock. That man's voice—it was like hearing Douglas Clayton speak again. And Doug's voice coming from that strange face, so unlike Doug in every way—it rocked me."

"Me, too," Doris admitted.

"You noticed it?"

Doris described the incident in Grand Central Station. She hadn't heard his voice then, but the way he held himself, the way he ran his fingers through his hair—she had thought, until he turned around and she saw his face, that it was really Doug.

Jane did not speak again until Doris stopped the car in front of the Blake house to let Leslie out. Then she said, "There's something queer about that man."

"How do you mean—queer?" Doris asked, a note of protest in her voice. "To my mind he's one of the best-looking human beings I've ever seen."

"I don't mean that." For once Jane's manner and voice were incisive. "You can't tell me coincidence goes that far. A man who talks like Doug and walks like him and uses his mannerisms and comes here, of all places, to work for the Company. I simply don't believe it."

"Don't you trust your own eyes?"

"There's something wrong about him," Jane insisted stubbornly. "Something terribly wrong. I wish he weren't coming to your house tonight, Leslie. I wish he weren't going to stay in Claytonville. All I say is—keep an eye on him."

AT six o'clock that evening Donald Shaw had finished shaving and he was reaching for a black tie when the telephone rang. He picked it up in some surprise. He was a stranger in Claytonville. No one was likely to call him.

"Shaw speaking."

"Oh, Shaw." The easy arrogance of the voice identified its owner at once. "Oliver Harrison speaking. Sorry to put you to work ahead of time and all that; I realize you won't be on my payroll until tomorrow."

My payroll. Donald Shaw's eyebrows rose in a questioning arc.

"But I know you won't mind. Some ass has mislaid all the notes for the job we're working on at the moment. I'd like you to try to find them tonight." Rapidly he described the papers to be looked for. "I've already telephoned the guard, who'll let you in and show you where the laboratory files are kept. Much obliged."

"Just a moment," Shaw said. "I'm sorry I can't help you out but I've accepted Miss Blake's invitation to a buffet supper at seven."

"That's all right. Don't give it a thought. I'll explain to her that I had a job for you to do. See you in the morning. Nine sharp, please." The telephone was replaced with a click.

For a long moment Shaw stared at his own telephone. Thoughtfully he set it down. Harrison hadn't wasted a moment in showing the new chemist clearly that he was in a subordinate position. He whistled soundlessly, running his fingers through his hair. Then he made up his mind. The Japanese wrestler had a clever trick of using his opponent's own strength to throw him. He grinned, put on his tie and adjusted his dinner jacket.

He ran down the stairs to the main floor of the inn. At the moment it appeared to be empty. The usual bevy of elderly women were still preparing for dinner. Then the door

herited the whole works. He's about a fifth cousin, I guess, and a good twenty years older than Doug. Funny how things work out, isn't it?"

"Is he a good man?" Shaw asked.

Swensen thought with his usual deliberation. "I'd say he is, on the whole. He expects a lot but he's fair enough. Far as I know, he's done his best. I hear he's raised the pay of the department heads and the other employees time and again, but never upped his own salary. Course, his wife's a gold mine and he don't need it." A pause. "They do say it's 'Yes, yes' at home with his missus."

"I suppose there have been a lot of changes."

"Some. The Company is growing fast. Needs new blood." Swensen watched sleepily while Shaw closed the third file drawer and looked around the room. "No luck?"

"The papers aren't in these files," Shaw answered. "That's for sure. Now where—" His eyes traveled from wall to wall.

"Want to let it go for the night?" the guard suggested. "Could be that Mr. High-and-Mighty Harrison slipped up for once."

Shaw shook his head. "No, I won't give up. I have a hunch that it would be a good idea to find the data, if it can be done. It won't be in a desk. Too obvious." He was thinking aloud now. He got up to open and then clap shut some large reference books. "If I were hiding those papers, I'd—" He broke off abruptly. "What about the locker room? Is that off bounds for newcomers?"

Swensen gave him a queer look of speculation. "Over in the main building," he said laconically. "Everybody checks in there. Always has. C'mon."

The two men left the laboratory, which the guard locked behind him, and they walked side by side to the main building. Again Swensen used his heavy bunch of keys, opened a door. "Room on the right."

The locker room was long and narrow, with the lockers in four rows, each bearing an employee's name. A wide ledge ran around the room on a level with the top of the door. Judging by a couple of forgotten hats and a package or two, it was used by the employees to hold miscellaneous items.

"When I was a kid," Shaw said, "I used to have a favorite hiding place. There was a wide shelf that extended out over my bedroom door, just like this one. No one ever thought of looking up there." He stretched out his arm, groped along the shelf over the top of the door, and pulled down a sheaf of blue papers.

"You—musta been quite a kid." Swensen's small eyes searched Shaw's face for a long time. A twinkle lurked in their depths.

"I had a friend who taught me most of the tricks I know. He was a great guy." Shaw grinned. Then he glanced at the first page and nodded. He handed the papers to Swensen. "I am turning these over to you for safekeeping. You can swear, if you have to, that I have not looked through them."

"I'll keep 'em in my pocket until I hand 'em over to Mr. Important Harrison in the morning." Swensen locked the door of the main building behind them. In the growing dusk he chuckled. "Seems like Harrison has met his match. But watch your step."

"I intend to," Shaw said grimly.

In a casual tone the guard added, "Speaking of steps, you've had an accident or something, haven't you? Act like you're too tired to crawl right now."

"I'm practically well. Just need to pick up a little more staying power. If I walk for more than half a mile, I seem to play out."

"Where's your car?"

"I don't own one."

"Tell you what," Swensen said, diving into a capacious pocket, "here's the key to my Chevy, that gray job over there. You can bring the heap back in the morning when you come to work. Just leave the key in it."

Shaw laughed. "Aren't you rather trusting with strangers for a guard?"

"It's not thieves the Company worries about. Smart guys like the Gypton people don't send out thugs. Easier to put in a trained chemist who knows what to look for."

The eyes of the men met in a flash of understanding. Then, before Donald Shaw could speak, the guard was off at a sturdy stride. At the corner of the building the big flashlight was switched on as Nors Swensen started back toward the laboratory.

vii

LESLIE turned for a final look in the mirror. As a rule, she spent only a minimum of time dressing, but tonight she found herself taking more trouble than usual, dissatisfied with her appearance, remembering Donald Shaw's eyes when they had rested on Jane Williams's face. They had revealed more than the normal admiration that Jane aroused. They had looked at her with a kind of rapt wonder.

For the first time in her life, Leslie was aware of a sense of rivalry. Not, she knew, that she could equal Jane's serene beauty. But Jane, after all, had made clear that she had no personal interest in Donald Shaw, not merely because he did not have the financial standing that she required; there was something more: a distrust, a kind of antipathy, almost a fear of this stranger.

"Something queer," she had said. "Something wrong." The voice, the gestures that reminded her of the man she had loved so long ago. *Something wrong.*

No one had ever accused Jane of being psychic. She had no imagination. This kind of reaction was not in the least typical of her and therefore it was the more disturbing.

Leslie saw the girl in the mirror who looked back at her, brows drawn together as she tried to cope with the puzzle. Then she remembered Donald Shaw's smile and her heart was warmed again. She dabbed perfume on her throat and at her temples, eying herself dubiously. "Well," she decided, "it's the best I can do."

She was all in soft greens, even to the corsage of orchids, which brought out the exquisite texture of her skin, the copper splinters in her hair and the amber lights in her eyes. A vivid lipstick accentuated the lovely curve of the sensitive mouth above her resolute dimpled chin.

A car door slammed as she ran downstairs, announcing the first arrivals. Agatha took up her station at the drawing room door. Tonight she was magnificent in a black lace dress,

47

a Parisian model that slimmed her large figure and accented its stateliness. She took a quick survey of her husband, immaculate in his dinner clothes, and turned to her stepdaughter. She nodded her approval.

"You really look very nice," she said.

Blake's hand rested lightly on his daughter's shoulder. "You're spring itself," he told her.

She smiled at him and leaned forward to kiss his cheek. Seeing the display of affection between father and daughter, Agatha turned away, her lips compressed.

The guests arrived almost together and Agatha passed them along with the speed of a practiced White House handshaker. They might, Leslie thought, have been so many robots on an assembly line. In contrast, Corliss Blake had a firm handshake and a personal greeting for everyone who passed him. Leslie herself, gay and natural and unselfconscious, had an intuitive awareness of how to make people feel at home. From top executive to stenographer, she welcomed them all with warm friendliness.

A smooth voice greeted Agatha. "You are queenly tonight."

"Dear Oliver!" she exclaimed, delighted. "How sweet of you. Oh, you must be Miss Allen."

Heads turned quickly. Jane's redheaded vixen was also in green, but a deep lustrous green that made her eyes glitter and her hair spectacular. The sleeveless, high-necked dress had a cape that swung over one shoulder and arm. Green satin slippers with high spiked heels made her seem unusually tall and slim.

"How kind of you to let me come, Mrs. Blake." She had a throaty contralto voice. The green eyes surveyed the room. "That dress of yours alone—"

Agatha, at the peak of her good humor, said, "Do let me present my husband, Miss Allen. And his righthand man, Mr. Harrison."

Miss Allen held out her hand to Corliss Blake, who bowed gravely. She said coolly, "How do you do, Mr. Harrison?"

Oliver gave her one of his attractive smiles. "Are you visiting here, Miss Allen?"

"Temporarily."

"Not on business then."

She smiled. "Business—always." The smile deepened.

Oliver moved on, exchanged a greeting with Blake and said a few words that Leslie did not catch. Then he was smiling down at her.

"You're beautiful," he told her, his voice pitched too low for her father to hear. "Save me most of the dances, won't you?"

"Hey," Paul Logan protested as he came up to them. "No unfair competition or I'll picket this joint."

Leslie laughed and turned to welcome Jane and Doris. Apparently, Jane had decided that she could cope with her competition. She wore sheer white and she had parted her hair in the middle, combing it smoothly to the sides, with a soft loose knot in back. No one else would have dared do it, but she looked like a madonna, with the lovely pure oval of her face and her big appealing blue eyes. On her right hand she wore Douglas Clayton's huge solitaire diamond and around her slim throat the double strand of matching pearls that had been her husband's wedding gift.

The waitress came in with a tray of small glasses of sherry. The guests had begun to form little groups. There was an unwritten law that members of one department were not to gather together, that office rank was abolished, and no business was ever discussed at the buffet suppers. As a result, there was an unusual degree of camaraderie among the personnel in all brackets.

Leslie, as usual, shook her head as the maid passed with the sherry. Her eyes moved around the room. Surely she could not have missed Donald Shaw's arrival. She slipped out into the hallway for a surreptitious look at the big grandfather clock. Seven-twenty. He wasn't coming!

She had moved quietly. That was how she happened to stumble on a curious scene. Felice Allen and Oliver Harrison stood side by side in the hall, engaged in a low-toned conversation. As the waitress offered the tray, Oliver reached carelessly for a glass, tipped it, and the liquid splashed over the lustrous green dress.

"Oliver! You stupid!" the girl snapped, her voice rising in an unexpectedly strident way, as though anger had stripped her of her pretensions to good breeding. "Look what you've done to my dress."

He reached for his handkerchief. "Sorry, Felice. But there's no point in making a scene. I'll pay the cleaning bill."

"I'll say you will! And the next time you reach for a glass, watch what you're doing. In fact," she added, with warning in her tone, "whatever you're reaching for—watch your step."

"I said I was sorry." There was no smooth charm in Oliver Harrison's voice now. "Cut it out!" He was suddenly savage, menacing.

Leslie turned quickly back to the drawing room, her head whirling. *Oliver. Felice.* And a few moments before they had met as total strangers. There had been something odd about that furtive meeting in the hall. And Oliver had said, when they watched Felice Allen enter the Fox and Rabbit, that he had never seen her before. Why on earth had he lied about it? And she had stared at him coolly, looked at his car, at the girl with him, and turned away. What were they playing at?

Agatha consulted her evening watch, whose face was concealed by a jeweled case in the shape of a flower. She signaled to Leslie. "Have you counted? We asked twenty-four tonight, including your extra guests and Miss Allen. I make it only twenty-three. Someone is missing but I think we'd better go ahead."

"It must be the new man, Shaw," her husband said. "Oliver explained to me when he came in. He asked Shaw to take care of something for him at the laboratory tonight." There was no expression in his voice.

"I don't see why Oliver didn't tell me himself," Agatha said in annoyance. "It's not at all like him. The most considerate man, as a rule! I've always thought that was one of his chief attractions. You know what I mean; he never forgets birthdays and things like that."

"I'll bet he's got a list," Paul muttered beside Leslie.

"Shsh," she warned him, caught her stepmother's eye and nodded. "We may as well lead the way," she said, and Paul joined her with alacrity.

The buffet suppers at the Blake house were justly famous in Claytonville. Tonight, there was a mommoth bowl of shrimp on ice with pungent cocktail sauce. There were smoked turkey, baked ham, salads of chicken and potato and fruit, tiny hot rolls, celery stuffed with cheese. Later there would be the dessert tray with choices of strawberry shortcake, ice cream or fresh fruit.

By custom, the guests found places for themselves at tables set for four. Paul tenderly balanced the plate that he had piled high with everything in sight. Leslie laughed as he deposited it safely with a sigh of relief.

"I always sample everything," he explained.

She looked at the size of the servings. "Sample?"

"This is nothing to what I could do if I really tried. The advantage of sampling everything is that there is no torment in choosing among those gourmet foods. When your stepmother loses 'my money,' she can always run a smorgasbord."

Before Leslie could comment, they were joined by a sulky Jane with one of the young clerks from the Company, a recent employee, a sandy-haired, shy young man who had previously attended only one of the Sunday suppers and was obviously unsure of himself. Leslie groped for his name. Mason. Jim Mason.

He set down his plate awkwardly, his uneasiness intensified by Jane's determination to ignore him.

"How nice to have you at my table, Mr. Mason," Leslie said with her warm smile.

"Th—thank you."

She introduced Paul Logan, whose good manners could always be depended upon. Jane deliberately tried to exclude young Mason from the conversation by devoting herself to Paul. She meant to make clear that her escort was not of her choosing and she found his presence intrusive. Paul, however, drew the newcomer into the talk deftly, deferred to his opinion, and probed to discover his chief enthusiasm, which turned out to be canoeing.

"Not that I get much chance to do it," Mason admitted, "but every year I spend a couple of weeks on a canoe trip. Last year in Canada. The year before I was on Lake Erie." Encouraged by Paul's apparent interest, he added rather boastfully, "Pretty rugged, I can tell you."

Jane's soft mocking laugh was like a blow. "Canoeing. Rugged!"

"It's easy to see, Jane," Paul said quickly, "that you haven't been on Lake Erie in a storm. They come without warning. It's the most shallow and therefore the most dangerous of the Great Lakes. I'd hate to attempt it myself."

The color that had flooded Mason's face receded. "You have to be careful, of course," he admitted. "You can't get too far from shore. Lately, I've been canoeing here on the river."

The big room had been filled with the buzz of conversation that indicates a successful party. Everyone seemed to be having a good time. Doris was the center of a gay quartet. Oliver Harrison, as usual, was paying assiduous court to Agatha. At another table Corliss Blake had been cornered by Felice Allen, who was questioning him about his work with deferential interest and a flattery to which he seemed to be impervious.

There fell one of those momentary lulls. The silence was broken by a deep, pleasant voice saying, "Mrs. Blake? I am your tardy and most repentant guest, Donald Shaw. I suppose Harrison explained that I might be late."

Agatha gave him her large but shapely hand, her bovine eyes surveying him from the clipped dark hair with its premature patches of white to the polished shoes.

"We are delighted to have you with us, Mr. Shaw." She

turned to Harrison. "As this is Mr. Shaw's first visit, Oliver, perhaps you'll take him to the buffet and then find him a table."

Oliver did not move. "I thought you would be working this evening, Shaw. The Company expects orders to be carried out."

There was a startled silence. Oliver Harrison had broken the cardinal rules: he had mentioned business, he had made clear the chasm between his job and that of his subordinate, and he had ticked off an employee publicly.

Leslie started to get up, spots of color burning in her cheeks. Her father forestalled her. He had already risen from his place at a nearby table. He came forward, holding out his hand.

"Glad to see you, Shaw. Sorry you were delayed."

"So am I," Shaw assured him. "It looks like a good party. Too bad to miss any of it."

Still too angry to realize that he was breaking the Blakes' rules of hospitality, Harrison said sharply, "So you couldn't find the data! I thought that I had made it clear that we must have it in the morning."

"Oh, yes, I found it," Shaw said cheerfully. "Darnedest thing, the way people can misplace papers, isn't it?"

Harrison's face stiffened. "Sure you got the right stuff?"

"According to the top page, it answered your description to a T. I didn't look through it, of course. Your guard Swensen was good enough to go along on the search and I turned it over to him for safekeeping."

Shaw returned Harrison's look steadily. "My trick, I think." Then he smiled, followed his host to the buffet, and joined the table that held only three people.

Oliver Harrison looked after him and his expression made Leslie's heart miss a beat. Felice Allen, too, had missed nothing of the exchange. The narrow green eyes flickered over Oliver's good-looking but stormy face in sardonic amusement and then she turned to watch Donald Shaw with alert speculation.

Aunt Agatha needn't worry about his being presentable, Leslie thought proudly. Like the man Flammonde in one of her favorite poems by Edwin Arlington Robinson, he

> . . . held his head
> Like one by kings accredited.

In any group he would be noticeable, with his height, his stern handsome face, his unselfconscious assurance. This was the quality for which Oliver strove in vain. His assurance was always marred by the arrogance that is a cover and a shield for insecurity and inferiority.

When the small tables had been cleared and the dessert tray passed, Doris went to preside over the coffee urn. Leslie excused herself.

"I'll have to check on the dance records. There wasn't time to sort them out this afternoon." She turned to the sandy-haired clerk, because she did not want to force Paul's hand. "Perhaps you'll help Miss Brooke by serving the coffee as she pours."

He looked wistfully at Jane, who ignored him. "Why I— I'm a clumsy guy—but I'd b-b-be glad—"

"I'll do it," Paul offered, and Leslie gave him a grateful smile.

She watched him go to the coffee table and saw Doris's face light up. In a few minutes they were chattering together in a confidential whisper. From their outraged looks at Oliver Harrison, they were evidently discussing their mutual indignation over his discourtesy to the new chemist.

When records had been stacked on the turntable, the guests drifted from the dining room to the sun room beyond the library, where rugs had been removed and the floor waxed to a high glaze.

Leslie turned to find Oliver beside her. "My dance," he said, and moved smoothly across the floor with her in his arms. He danced, as he did everything, competently and easily. At length he became aware of her silence. He held her a little away from him, looking down at her with a smile.

"What's wrong?" he asked. "Tired?"

"Angry," she told him honestly. "What on earth made you so rude, so—so domineering, so insolent, to Mr. Shaw?"

"You don't understand business," he said, as though he were addressing with patience a somewhat dull child. "He's to be in my department, you know. I handle it my own way."

"We don't entertain employees," she said hotly. "Only guests. *Our* guests. Please remember that another time."

"You seem to take a great deal of interest in Shaw," Harrison answered. He was still smiling but his expression disturbed her.

She did not reply, thinking that her silence might underline her reproof. They turned, swayed, moved to the rhythm of the dance band. She saw Doris dancing with Paul, her black eyes snapping, both of them laughing as they tried out some new steps. Donald Shaw stood against the wall, for a moment, running his fingers through his hair, his gray eyes searching.

Then he made straight for Jane Williams, spoke to her, held out his hand. At first, she seemed to hesitate and then she nodded. She wasn't a woman who could tolerate being a wallflower, even for a single dance, even if she had to accept a partner whom she disliked. They danced, her big blue eyes looking up at him with just that touch of appealing admiration so deadly to the male.

While Leslie was claimed by one partner after another, Donald Shaw and Jane Williams remained together, sometimes dancing, sometimes sitting in deep chairs in the library beyond. At length, Oliver cut in and danced away with Jane. Now, Leslie thought, now at last he'll come to me. Instead, Shaw stopped beside Doris. They chatted for a moment and then they strolled out on the terrace. Leslie turned away rather blankly. If he couldn't have Jane, at least he could talk to her young sister.

As Paul cut in on Oliver, Felice Allen stretched out a hand to the latter and spoke to him. Apparently not having heard her, he went on, and she spoke again, sharply. He turned back and led her out on the floor, his face like a thundercloud.

The record stopped, another dropped down, there was the languorous throbbing rhythm of a tango. Except for Corliss Blake and his daughter, everyone was dancing; even Agatha, who towered over Jim Mason as he strode around the room as though launched on a fifty-mile walk, using Agatha's right arm like the handle of the town pump. After one dance with his wife, Blake always sat out the rest.

For the first time in her young and popular life, Leslie found herself at a dance without a partner. She told herself that the room was too hot, that she needed fresh air; and she stepped out on the terrace. If she had another reason, who was she, after all, to be so much wiser than other girls?

At the far end of the terrace, a man and a girl sat perched on the stone wall, the man's face lighted now and then as he drew on a cigarette, the girl's voice chattering eagerly.

". . . and if she's not in love," Leslie heard the Babbling Brooke say, "at least she's at the crossroads. Everyone in town expects . . ."

Leslie turned back to the overheated room. The record came to an end. It was a relief to hear the little bustle that indicated the guests were preparing to leave. She joined her father and stepmother at the door. Surely now—

Donald Shaw had almost reached her. " . . . at the pool," Doris called him. "Web Rock. Don't forget."

Felice Allen laid her hand on Shaw's arm. "You're at

the Fox and Rabbit, too, aren't you? Perhaps you'll be kind enough to take me back."

He was gone, after thanking the Blakes for a delightful evening.

NATURE loves to play tricks for the bewilderment and consternation of the weather forecasters. The next morning, with a forecast of cloudy and cooler, was hot and breathless. The sun came scorching out of a cloudless sky. Leaves drooped motionless on maple and elm and walnut trees. The river sparkled blindingly but there was not a ripple. It was the kind of day that heralds a storm.

Even in a sleeveless blouse and tailored shorts, Leslie found the big attic room that she had turned into a studio scorching. The large skylight could not be opened and it seemed to attract and hold the sun's relentless heat. She opened the small casement windows under the eaves and sent Rosie in search of electric fans.

For an hour she puttered around, straightening the studio, which she had not entered for months except to renew the damp cloths that kept the clay moist.

Incorrigibly honest, she finally made herself confess that she was not really thinking about the task that she had set herself, that she was wholly absorbed in brooding about the man who had not asked her to dance the night before, the man who had seemed literally unable to tear himself away from Jane Williams.

"I'm ashamed of you, Leslie Blake," she told herself firmly, "mooning like a lovesick schoolgirl. Haven't you any pride at all? If he likes someone better than he does you, hold up your head and forget about him. Now you get to work, young woman."

Her own crisp words, spoken aloud in the quiet studio, made her laugh at herself. She got out a sketchbook and set herself to planning the statue that was to memorialize Douglas Clayton's heroic action.

At first, she made idle, meaningless marks with charcoal. There was one sure thing. She'd had only that brief glimpse of his face in the film. It was queer how distinctly she remembered it. But she needed more detail in order to create a real likeness. And even if Jane still had any photographs, she had made clear that she had no intention of going to the trouble of producing them.

What then? Almost of its own accord the charcoal began to move across the paper, as though independent of her fingers, of her will, sketching a man spread-eagled against a cliff, groping for a handhold as he pulled himself up.

At length, Leslie sat back to look at her sketch. She felt the lifting of the heart, the exhilaration that comes— so rarely!—with a sense of creative achievement, of having grasped and made tangible a private vision. The lines were spare and sure. There was something infinitely lonely in the figure of the man who pulled himself upward, a suggestion of shrinking of the body from the impact of possible gunfire, and yet an unshaken will that could carry him over the top to face whatever might await him there.

It's good, Leslie thought in a kind of wonder. It's really good. She had forgotten everything now but the work in hand. Rapidly she set up her armature, dragged the big keg of wet clay beside her, perched on a high stool, picked up a small piece of clay and worked it between her fingers.

There were running feet on the stairs and Doris came in. "Hi, Leslie! Whew! It's hot in here! I had a wonderful time last night. You were a love to ask Paul especially for me."

She threw herself on a rickety couch against the wall, fanning herself vigorously with a newspaper she had picked up, and went on without giving Leslie time to speak. The Babbling Brooke rippled gaily along.

"I've got my work cut out for me, I can see that, Paul's more in love with you than I realized. But I managed to get in a few good licks."

Leslie, pressing clay onto the armature, began to laugh.

"Laugh all you like," Doris said cheerfully, "but I'm not the girl to let grass grow under her feet or to gather any moss, I can tell you. In fact, I staked my claim."

"How did you do that?" Leslie asked in a tone of affectionate amusement.

"Oh, not to his face, of course. Actually, the one I told was the stunning and mysterious stranger in our midst, Mr. Shaw."

"Mr. Shaw!" For a moment Leslie's hand was motionless, then she reached mechanically for more clay. "What on earth has he to do with it?"

"Well, it's like this. He asked me to dance but I could see he was awfully tired so I suggested that we sit out on the terrace."

I saw you. Leslie was relieved to discover that she had not spoken the words aloud.

"Well, we got talking. One thing and another. He mentioned you. Said he'd picked you up and taken you to the Country Club. Said Paul had thanked him for rescuing his girl. So," Doris said firmly, "I told him Paul was mine. Only he doesn't know it yet."

"Why on earth," Leslie asked, trying to sound unconcerned, "did he speak of me?"

"I don't know. Just idle chatter. You know how it is. So that's when I said Paul was mine and I thought you'd probably marry Oliver Harrison."

"You—what!"

"Not exactly. I just said if you weren't actually in love yet you were certainly at the crossroads, and everyone expected you to marry him, sooner or later."

"Honestly, Doris, sometimes you say the most irresponsible things."

"There's nothing to get excited about. It was just one of those casual comments. You know how it is. And, anyhow, he probably won't even remember it, if that's what is bothering you. And it won't get back to Oliver Harrison through him. I don't think our Mr. Shaw is feeling friendly enough at this point to indulge in any personal gossip with him. That is, if he ever really says anything personal. He doesn't give away a thing about himself. Courteous and pleasant, but he presents you with a blank wall in the nicest way in the world."

Doris sat bolt upright, her black eyes snapping. "Did you ever hear anything like the way Oliver Harrison spoke to him? 'The Company expects orders to be carried out.' I'd like him to be carried out. For a moment I honestly hoped your father would tell him what he thought of him. But he—" Her voice trailed off and she did not look at Leslie.

The latter kept her eyes on the armature. She, too, had hoped that her father would reprimand Oliver in some way for his discourtesy, although, for a reason she could not understand, he usually gave Oliver his own way without protest. His attitude toward his head chemist obscurely troubled Leslie.

For a moment she was tempted to tell Doris about that curious scene between Oliver and Felice Allen, which she had accidentally witnessed. Something very queer there. They knew each other, seemed to know each other well, but they were pretending to be strangers.

Leslie checked her confidence. Doris was staunch and loyal but she was still the Babbling Brooke. Everything she knew or heard came pouring out, sooner or later, though it was never done in malice.

"Speaking of Mr. Shaw," Doris went on, "that man has gone off the deep end about Jane. Brother! Did you notice the way he was right beside her every chance he got all evening long?"

For a moment Doris's volatile gaiety was dampened. "You know, Leslie, I can't help wondering if Jane is right about him. When she said that something was wrong, I mean. She has always attracted men but I never knew one to go down for the count that way. First sight and everything. Especially without a scrap of encouragement from Jane. I got to thinking about it last night. Of course, Jane is not only beautiful; she's a darned wealthy widow and he doesn't seem to have a penny of his own."

Leslie packed more clay on the armature, working as though her life depended on it. Without looking up, she asked, "How does Jane feel about him now?"

"That's just the point, the reason I came over here this morning. I wanted to get away from Jane, away from Web Rock. Honestly, I've never seen her like this. Like a wild woman."

"Jane!"

"Last night she went home in a regular daze and when I asked her what was wrong she snapped, 'Oh, stop talking!' and she was pacing her floor till all hours. And that's not the worst."

Doris jumped up and began to wander restlessly around the studio. "This morning she was up before eight, and you know how she hates early hours. I heard the most terrible racket going on and found her in that big storage room going through old trunks and barrels and boxes. She had stuff scattered all over the floor."

Leslie lifted a puzzled face. "Why on earth?"

"That's what I wanted to know. She said she was looking for those old pictures of Douglas Clayton. She said something about this man Shaw driving her crazy; he's so much like Doug, so much unlike him. She has a wild idea in her head, a kind of double cross he may be working at the Company. Then when she finally had all the pictures spread out, we looked them over together. I think she was awfully relieved when she saw for herself that the resemblance was in manners and voice and carriage and not in his features, except that his eyes are the same, of course."

She handed Leslie a snapshot. "Jane said I could give you this one if you still want it. Really it's the best of Doug,

better than the big cabinet photographs, but Jane doesn't
like it because it's poor of her. The camera caught her with
her mouth open and she looks sort of stupid."

For a long time Leslie studied the snapshot. A young
man and a girl were sitting on the ground with a picnic
basket in front of them. Jane was easily recognizable, a younger Jane with clothes that were ten years out of date, her
hair curled and fluffed around her head. She was looking
at Douglas Clayton and, as Doris had said, she appeared
rather stupid with her mouth open.

Douglas Clayton. It was hard to believe this was the same
man who, only a few months later, had clawed his way
up a mountain, gaunt, with somber eyes. He was looking
at the camera, a laughing, carefree, happy young man, little
more than a boy, with a boy's sensitive mouth and the open
trusting friendliness of a person who has encountered little
if any cruelty or injustice in his life.

"You can see for yourself," Doris pointed out, "there's
no real resemblance to Mr. Shaw, except height and coloring,
and his mannerisms, of course. That's what made Jane so
suspicious."

"Suspicious? But why? Of what?"

"Well, you remember that article about fake heirs she was
reading. She's got a crazy theory that our mysterious stranger
has come here to try to establish himself as Doug. She thinks
he might have known Doug somewhere, perhaps in the service, studied his ways and all that. And ten years make a lot
of difference in the way people look."

"I think Jane is as mad as a hatter," Leslie said flatly.
She smoothed the clay with a rotary motion of her thumb.

"I kind of hope so," Doris admitted. "Mr. Shaw is a real
charmer but, for his own sake, the sooner he gets over this
infatuation for Jane, the better for all concerned. She—it
sounds silly but I think she's afraid of him and yet attracted
at the same time. Or maybe," Doris commented with the
shrewdness that always surprised Leslie, "that's why Jane is
afraid. Just because she is attracted. Jane hasn't ever let herself be emotionally involved, whatever she may say about
Doug now that he is gone. What I think is, if you love a man
you'd jump at the chance to go to the Sahara Desert or any
hell hole with him."

Leslie turned the armature, reached for more clay, and
began to press it into place.

"Do you think Rosie would make us some iced coffee?"
Doris asked.

Leslie started to get up. "Of course. I'll ask her."

"No, you go on working. I'll do it." Doris ran down the stairs.

Leslie sat looking at the snapshot. *Something wrong. A very wealthy widow. Afraid but attracted. Fake heirs.* What had Donald Shaw said to her? That if he really had been Douglas Clayton she and her father would be in an awkward position.

Doris was back again and handed her a tall cold glass. In the interim she had apparently forgotten her distrust of Donald Shaw and her volatile mind had seized on another subject.

"Leslie, are you really interested in Oliver Harrison?"

"Not for one single minute," Leslie assured her in a tone that impelled belief.

Doris breathed a long sigh of satisfaction. "Jeepers, I'm glad! I'd hate to have anything come between us. You're my very best friend and I never could replace you. But if you were to marry The Great Profile—"

"You got that from Paul," Leslie accused her.

"Talking about me behind my back," Paul said from the doorway. He stood grinning at them. "Accusing me of—what exactly? I warn you in advance I'm going to deny it. Hey, my need is greater than yours. Women and children last." Coolly he took Doris's glass of iced coffee and began to drink it.

"I called Oliver Harrison The Great Profile," Doris explained.

"That was just a minor effort," Paul said modestly. "Now if I really let myself go about the Viking god—"

"Well, don't," Leslie warned him.

"Hey, you haven't really fallen for the guy, have you?"

"He's part of the Company," Leslie reminded him. "Dad made it a family rule long ago: no gossip about the personnel."

"Gossip?" Paul tried to sound shocked and injured, in spite of his broad smile. "Does it hurt that guy if I say he enters a room like Caesar stalking to the Forum? A fair tribute, that's all."

Leslie tried not to laugh, failed. "Stop it, Paul."

"Whatever you say," he agreed with suspicious humility. He looked at the armature with its padding of clay. "Now if that were Harrison, you'd have to give him a toga and a wreath of vine leaves for his head."

Doris laughed in delight.

"You are impossible, both of you," Leslie said firmly.

"It's the heat and not my intentions. What a day to stay cooped up in an attic."

Leslie, working busily, made no comment. Paul lounged against the door.

"There's shade from the willows down by the river," he said musingly. "The water is cool. That barge is dandy to dive from. And—guess what?—my bathing trunks just happen to be in the car."

Leslie laughed. "You win. Paul, you can change in the small guest room. Doris, you'll find suits in my room. I'll just get some wet towels to wrap around the armature and then I'll join you."

When she had changed to a white bathing suit, she ran across the lawn, down to the river. Paul was already in the water. Doris, sitting on the barge, let her legs dangle over the side. She waved her arm and called something. Leslie pulled off her cap so she could hear.

"What?"

"We've got company. How did you get here, you little monster?"

Jack Williams was sitting on the grass. His face was flushed and his manner defiant. "I walked."

"Does your mother know where you are?"

"She never minds my coming to see Leslie. It's all right, isn't it, Leslie?"

"Just fine," she assured him. She looked at his bathing trunks. "But so far you've just been practicing," she warned him. "You can't swim yet and the river is much deeper than the pools you've been in."

"He can't go in the water," Doris protested. "He's supposed to be home in bed. He had a fever this morning."

"Aw, Aunt Doris, don't be mean!"

Paul had come up on the lawn. "Hi, Sheriff," he said, "have you caught any cattle thieves this morning?"

"I'm not a sheriff today. I'm a pirate." Jack looked wistfully from face to face. "Can't I swim *atall*? I'm so hot."

Leslie touched his cheek lightly. "So you are. I'll tell you what. We'll all sit on the barge for a while and play pirate."

"Jeepers!"

"And then," Leslie went on, "Aunt Doris will drive you home and you'll go back to bed so you can get over the fever and come swimming with us. Promise?"

"Cross my heart," Jack said solemnly.

So for an hour they played pirate with a small boy. Or rather, they told pirate stories and he was content to sit quietly, curled up at Leslie's feet, listening in wide-eyed delight. It was at moments like these that Leslie realized how very much she liked Paul. He treated Jack as though he were his contemporary, without any of the condescension by which grown-ups so often insult children, entering the imaginary game unselfconsciously and with zest.

"I betcha," Jack said, "if we had grappling irons we could fasten this old barge to an enemy ship and board her in about two minutes. I betcha we could."

"Would you make the prisoners walk the plank, Captain Blood?" Doris asked.

He considered the problem with the seriousness it merited. "No. Long as we haven't any motor, I'd get oars and make 'em all galley slaves."

"How you going to divide the loot, Captain?" Paul asked.

"Half for me, 'cause I'm the Captain. The rest equally among my crew, except maybe Leslie would get a little bit more."

"I like that," Doris said in pretended indignation. "You should never play favorites, Captain. First thing you know, you'll have a mutiny on your hands."

"Well, just a teeny bit more. Because, after all, she's Leslie." He tipped back his head to look at her with adoration in his eyes.

Leslie fought back her temptation to bend over and kiss the small face, so flushed with fever, but she knew it would be an insult to the dignity and the prestige of Captain Blood.

"Aye, aye, Captain. How shall we dispose of our loot?"

"The usial way."

"Usual," Doris corrected.

"That's what I said. Usial. The usial thing is to bury it somewhere, I guess. Paul, could you be a pirate in a canoe?"

"I never heard of one," Paul admitted.

"I just wondered. Lots of nights, just before it's quite dark, a canoe goes up and down the river. I just wondered if it was a real pirate, spying out the land, sort of."

Paul grinned at Leslie. "That sounds like our intrepid friend Mason. No, Captain Blood, I doubt if he is a pirate."

Jack relinquished the idea with a sigh of disappointment. "It would of been sort of interesting. A pirate in a canoe is not usial. You know what I betcha? I betcha if real pirates had this barge they'd fill it with pine knots and tar and ram it against a ship so's it would burn right down."

Leslie touched Jack's cheek lightly, looked at Doris in alarm. The latter scrambled to her feet. "I'll change right away and take you home, little monster. Time you were back in bed."

"Aw, Aunt Doris!"

"You promised," Leslie reminded him softly.

He got up without further protest, leaned dizzily against her. "Awful hot, isn't it?"

Paul scooped him up in his arms. "It sure is. Much too hot. With your permission, Captain Blood, the crew will go off duty."

"Awright," Jack said thickly. His head rested against Paul's shoulder. He closed his eyes.

ix

BY that night, Jack's fever had rocketed sky-high. The doctor diagnosed his trouble as a severe attack of influenza. In spite of his efforts and Jane's frantic telephone calls, there was no nurse to be had, and Jack proved to be a restless patient who had to be watched constantly to keep him in bed.

In an emergency it never occurred to anyone to look to Jane Williams for help. That, indeed, was the time when she required the most attention and consideration for herself. She simply couldn't watch Jack night and day, she complained fretfully. Her nerves wouldn't stand it. Why did things like this have to happen to her?

It never occurred to anyone to make the obvious answer: "Why not? They happen to everyone else."

Doris and Leslie took over the nursing, Doris during the day and Leslie at night. Rather than go back and forth, Leslie packed a bag and moved to Web Rock. The ten days she spent there seemed, in retrospect, to have a dreamlike quality: the silent night duty in the dim room with its shaded lamp; the restlessness of the sick child and, worse, the time when he lay in a stupor and did not stir at all. In the course of those long hours Leslie's devotion to the child grew in proportion to his need of her and the help and comfort she was able to give him. For the first time, too, she began to realize how much she wanted children of her own.

Those silent vigils, when she was the only person awake in the house, perhaps in the whole dark village, became a time for searching her own heart, coming to terms with herself as a human being, knowing and accepting both her strength and her weakness.

At eight in the morning, Doris would come up to take her place and Leslie would go down to the terrace, where her breakfast tray had been prepared. Jane, of course, rarely appeared before ten. Leslie would eat chilled melon and hot flaky muffins and sip scalding hot coffee. Then she would stretch out on a long wicker chair, looking up at the green leaves of the trees, out on the bright flower beds, down at the oval pool where Jane's pink water lilies floated. After that, in a darkened guestroom she slept deeply until mid-afternoon.

Every day Agatha sent over her mail and relayed her telephone messages. Except for that, Leslie was completely out of touch with her home. The dangerous illness of a small boy had crowded everything else out of sight. Now and then she thought of her sculpture, realizing that she probably would not have time to finish it and have it cast before the Clayton Festival.

On a Saturday, ten days after she had taken up her nursing duties, Leslie awakened in the afternoon to find Doris beaming down at her.

"Dr. Fletcher is here. He says Jack is out of the woods. He's going to be just fine. Tomorrow he can sit up and the next day he can go out of doors for a little while. We nurses are discharged." She leaned over to kiss Leslie's cheek, still flushed from sleep. "We owe it to you. I'll never forget it, Les. Never in this world."

"You needn't thank me, Doris. Honestly. I really love Jack and I wanted to do it. He's such a little darling." She stretched like a cat. "I'll take a bath and pack and go home right away."

"Why don't you get into a swim suit and come down to the pool? You haven't had a single scrap of fun all the time you've been here." Doris grinned. "I suppose I should not think of urging you, because Paul is down there. Unfair competition."

"Idiot! But I would enjoy a swim."

The two girls, Doris in a red swim suit, Leslie in pale green, found half a dozen people congregated at the pool, some swimming, some sprawled lazily on chairs on the lawn. Jane, in a black suit that set off her fair hair, was dividing her attention between Donald Shaw and Dr. Fletcher, the attractive young child specialist, a widower, who had recently set up practice in Claytonville. The two men were the only ones who were not dressed for swimming.

Paul waved from the pool as he caught sight of Leslie. "Hi, there, Florence Nightingale."

Dr. Fletcher and Donald Shaw had risen as the girls came out. The doctor smiled at Leslie. "I haven't thanked my faithful night nurse yet. You've done a splendid job, Miss Blake."

"I'm so happy to know that Jack is recuperating nicely," she said.

you would like. I've been willing, glad, to use my own money
for—" The big bovine eyes quickened. "Is that it? Is it my
money? You've minded about my having my own money?"

"It's not that," Leslie said slowly. "Of course we haven't
minded. But, somehow, it always comes up: 'My own money.'
As though—as though you thought it could buy anything. I
don't mean to be rude, to hurt you, Aunt Agatha. Honestly.
It's not that you aren't generous with it. But we can't ever
forget it. You won't let us."

"But you see," Agatha Blake said, "it is all I ever had to
give either of you. My money. So I wanted it to be important to you, to make up—"

"Make up?"

Agatha concluded with difficulty. "Make up for the love
that neither of you could ever give me."

Leslie caught her breath, feeling the older woman's pain,
aware of her as she had never been before. The idea that
Agatha Blake, below that placid surface, had depths of
emotion had never crossed her mind. How blind, how self-
absorbed she must have been all these years!

"Do you know how I happened to marry your father?"
Agatha asked. "He adored your mother. She and I were
friends. In a way, she was the only close friend I ever had. I
don't seem to have the capacity to make friends, though I've
tried so hard. They were married when we met. I always
loved Corliss, but, of course, he didn't know. He wouldn't
have been interested anyhow; he was so absorbed in your
mother. I don't blame him and I wouldn't have had it other-
wise. You mustn't misunderstand that. She was the loveliest
person I ever knew."

For the first time, Leslie looked at her stepmother with
an awakening of understanding and sympathy. There was no
self-pity in Agatha, only a kind of bewilderment.

"All the time she was ill I was there to look after her;
then after she died and Corliss lost almost all interest in life
for a time, I looked after you. I got to be a sort of habit.
He knew I'd be good to you and he had no love to give to
any other woman. I understood that. But at least—he was
there. He has always been very kind," she went on flatly, "but
I made a mistake, didn't I?"

Leslie blinked back tears. "Neither of us could get along
without you," she declared.

Agatha's face warmed. "You mean that?"

Leslie nodded. "It will be all right, Aunt Agatha." The
dimple flashed in her chin. "Why don't you try Jane Williams's
trick? It's devastating with men. Don't attempt to help Dad.
Let him help you. Some people can get their happiness only

by giving. And don't offer him a cent, even if you see him selling apples from a pushcart on the street."

To their mutual surprise, Agatha began to laugh. "Not a cent," she agreed. She looked at her watch. "Will you be home for dinner?"

"Home for keeps," Leslie told her.

"I'm glad," Agatha said simply.

*   *   *

It was not until he appeared for dinner that Leslie noticed the change in her father. He had welcomed her home, said she looked tired and he hoped she'd get some rest, and then he fell silent, brooding over his meal, eating very little. Once Agatha opened her lips to urge him to eat, and then closed them firmly. Leslie winked at her. None the less, something was wrong.

He would have his coffee in his study, he decided. He had some work to do.

"Dad," Leslie said when he started to leave the room.

He turned to smile at her. "Nice to have you home again, dear. I've missed you." He went quickly into his study and closed the door to forestall any questions.

When Leslie opened the door a few minutes later, she found him sitting at his desk, a letter spread out before him, his eyes fixed unseeingly on the window. She curled up at his feet, her head resting against his knee. She did not speak. After a few minutes of silence he stretched out his hand to stroke her soft copper curls.

"Is it anything you can tell me?" she asked at length.

"Company business," he said. "You wouldn't understand. Anyhow, I don't want you to worry."

She tipped back her head to smile at him. "But we're family," she reminded him.

"So was the Company," he said in a tired voice, "or at least I tried to make it so. A team working happily together."

"And you've succeeded, Dad. Everyone says that."

"I thought so, too. But it looks as though I'd been mistaken. Somewhere, Leslie, I've made a bad mistake. Perhaps an irrevocable mistake."

She waited quietly for him to go on. He picked up the letter, read it in silence, handed it to her. It was from the Gypton people of whom she had heard, making an offer for the new formula the Clayton Textile Company was developing. Unaccustomed as she was to business phraseology, Leslie was aware that it was an oddly phrased letter.

She read it twice. "You're right, Dad. I don't understand. What's wrong with it?"

He took back the letter. "To begin with, the offer they make is preposterous. It's so inadequate that it is ludicrous, insulting."

"But, after all, you don't need to sell to them, do you?"

"This is a very cagily worded letter, Leslie. They probably had their lawyer go over every single word. A very tricky letter, a threatening letter. What they are saying between the lines is that they will pay this token price—or else; that they already have most of the data about the formula and they can get the rest without any difficulty."

"But how can they get it?" Leslie asked.

"Somewhere," her father told her grimly, "we have a traitor in the Company. That's the only possible explanation."

"Dad!" Leslie sat bolt upright, staring at him in disbelief and horror.

"That's why I said I had made a mistake. There is only one newcomer working in the research laboratory and that is Shaw. He was my choice. And yet, I'd have staked anything on the man's integrity." He laughed without amusement. "In a sense I did stake everything. I don't know chemistry, but I thought I knew men."

His fist crashed on the desk, startling her. "I don't see how my judgment could have been so completely at fault. And yet from the beginning Harrison has disliked and distrusted the man." He crushed the letter into a ball, smoothed it out again. "Well," he said heavily, "if Gypton gets the formula I'll resign from the Company. I'm not fit to be in charge. Harrison can step into my shoes, and I suspect that he has been waiting for that."

He rested his hand lightly on Leslie's shoulder. "In a way, that might be best for the Company, anyhow. I've tried to handle it as Douglas Clayton wanted it handled but it has never been a congenial task."

"What would you have preferred to do if you hadn't had to earn a living and had not inherited his estate?"

"I'd like to work for world peace. That seems to me the most important, the most vital and pressing job a man could do. But, of course, if I feel I must resign from the Company, I couldn't in honor keep Clayton's money and his property. You see that? So I'd have to begin earning a living in a different way. I've been thinking that, if worst comes to worst, I can go back to my old job."

"You were a good architect, Dad."

"But times change, you know. The firm I was with devotes

all its time at present to big housing developments, bidding for contracts—making deals, more often than not. It's not the way it was a few years ago, when we were designing small private homes for individuals. And on my own—I'm not a young man. Heaven knows how long it would be before I could support you and Agatha decently."

"That's not important," Leslie assured him eagerly. "There's no place in this busy world for idle women any more. There are lots of jobs and, so far as I'm concerned, I'd be interested in the challenge of seeing what I can do."

"I'm proud of my daughter," he said huskily.

She leaned her arms on his knee, smiling up at him. "I'm proud of my father. Deeply proud. But, Dad, before you do anything drastic you'll make very sure, won't you?"

"Sure of what?"

"Sure that you know beyond doubt that there is a traitor in the Company and that you know who he is."

"But the only—"

"Dad, I don't believe Donald Shaw is dishonest. I think you were right about him in the first place. There must be someone else."

"You can't judge, dear. You barely know him."

"There must be someone else," she insisted. "There simply has to be."

He looked down at her intently, saw the color that flushed her cheeks while her eyes met his steadily.

"You—like him," he said with an effort. "Is that it?"

"I love him," she said simply. "I just this minute realized it."

"Oh, Leslie." His arm drew her closer to him. He looked over her head with troubled eyes. "Poor baby."

After a long time he said, "Before I met your mother I fell in love with a girl who came to visit in town one summer. She was unlike any girl I'd ever known. Pretty, sophisticated— and mysterious. That was the charm. No one really knew anything about her, what she was or where she came from. I mooned around her for months, making a complete fool of myself, and when she finally eloped with a married man twice her age I thought my life was ruined."

He chuckled. "There's something about mystery that is irresistible. But it won't do for everyday living. In the long run we don't thrive on moonlight; we need bread and butter."

"Was my mother bread and butter?"

Corliss Blake was silent for a moment. "No," he said slowly, "she wasn't bread and butter, but she wasn't moonlight either. She was the sun shining on the Garden of Eden."

He stood up, drawing his daughter in the circle of his arm.

They stood looking across the lawn to the river. A canoe went silently by in the dusk.

"Jim Mason," Leslie said. She laughed softly. "Jack Williams thinks he's a pirate spying out the land."

"Mason," her father repeated, a note of startled alertness in his voice. "Mason."

"What about him?"

"It just occurred to me. He's another fairly recent employee. Perhaps—"

"Dad, do you think he could possibly be the one?"

"We'll see. There must be no more mistakes. This time I must be very sure. Now you had better get to bed and rest after your nursing. I'll tell Rosie not to disturb you in the morning. Good night, dear."

"Good night." Leslie kissed him and yawned widely.

Before getting into bed she stood for a minute at her window. It was almost dark, but a darker shadow moved noiselessly along the river. Jim Mason was returning, drops of water glistening in the moonlight as he lifted his paddle.

✖

DONALD SHAW, too, was thinking about Jim Mason. In the two weeks he had worked for the Clayton Textile Company he had scarcely been aware of the shy young clerk from the accounting department beyond seeing him occasionally in the Company restaurant. There had been too much to occupy his thoughts.

In the first place, he had plunged at once into work in the research laboratory. It had taken only a few days to make clear how revolutionary the next textile would be. Its effect on almost all the standard fabrics on the market would be enormous. *If* the formula proved to be satisfactory. *If* it could be marketed properly. *If* the secret could be retained by the Company.

Those were sobering *ifs*. The chances that the new textile could be produced and distributed satisfactorily often seemed remote. The weight, the power of the Gypton organization were such that it had long dominated the field.

None the less, there was an enthusiasm and faith among the research chemists, a daily excitement about the work they were doing, that sometimes made Shaw believe that sheer loyalty and wholehearted devotion to the job could achieve what unscrupulous power could not do.

There was only one weak spot in the laboratory. That was the attitude of the men toward Oliver Harrison, the head chemist. There wasn't, as far as Shaw could see, a single chemist who really liked him. His arrogance, his offensive manner of issuing orders, his immoderate vanity and unbridled ambition, which made him try to assume full personal credit for the work of the group, all this caused constant tension and irritation.

On the other hand, Harrison was a fine chemist. No one could deny that, though the initial research had not been his; indeed, the formula had been taking final shape, as the result of the work of a chemist now dead, before Harrison ever

74

entered the Company, less than a year before. Even so, his energy and determination to see it succeed had provided a great stimulus.

For all his dislike and distrust of the man, Shaw was forced in honesty to respect his abilities. Their own relationship was a strange one. Harrison made no attempt to conceal his dislike of Shaw and his determination to grasp the first excuse to fire him. But never since the night of the Blakes' buffet had either man referred to the papers that Harrison had concealed and ordered Shaw to find.

In some ways, Shaw thought the situation had its ridiculous aspects. There were times when he was tempted to say, "Look here, what were you trying to accomplish by that silly performance?" Something kept him silent. He would bide his time. And yet he had an uncomfortable feeling that time was running out. Rumors of the formula were widespread throughout the industry. Somewhere in the Company was an employee who was slipping out information. But who?

Because of his dislike for Harrison, Shaw would have liked to believe him the guilty man, but there were other factors. Harrison was ambitious but not, Shaw thought, for money alone. What he wanted was power; he wanted to head the Clayton Company. In that case, he would be the last man to betray it.

Only a few days earlier, Shaw had been eating lunch with one of the laboratory chemists. Harrison had entered the Company restaurant and moved toward a choice corner table by the window. At the same time Jim Mason had approached it. Harrison had brushed past him, almost shoving him out of the way, and pulled out a chair. For a moment the sandy-haired accountant had stood stock still, looking at him, such naked hatred in his green eyes that Shaw was startled. Then Mason had turned away and pulled out a chair at another table.

Shaw might almost have thought he imagined that look if the chemist with him had not given a low whistle. "Whew! Did you see that? Mason looked as though he'd like to stick a knife in Harrison."

"Yes, I noticed," Shaw said quietly.

The chemist, a pleasant young man named Wilcox, with blunt features and an air of unconquerable good humor, shot him a quick look. "What goes on around here? This used to be the most congenial outfit I was ever in. Now there's Mason looking as if he would like to throttle Harrison, and Harrison acting most of the time as though he would like nothing better than to slug you."

Shaw laughed. "Just the hot weather. It takes some people like that. Wait until we get a cool spell and they will relax."

"Maybe," Wilcox said skeptically. "I noticed that the heat doesn't seem to affect you. So far, you've taken everything Harrison handed out without even turning a hair. And yet I wouldn't put you down as an easy mark. Not like poor Blake."

Shaw's eyebrows rose in a question. "Poor Blake?"

"A good guy," the chemist said hastily. "Don't misunderstand me. One of the best. But he certainly lets Harrison take over the driver's seat." He repeated with a troubled look, "But he's a good guy."

Shaw was troubled, too. It became more and more evident that Harrison was steadily taking over the reins from Corliss Blake and that Blake wasn't even putting up a fight. Shaw suspected that his fellow chemist shared his doubt, wondered whether Blake could be selling out information on the formula to the Gypton people.

He tried to dismiss the idea but he could not help remembering that Blake had married a woman of great wealth whom, rumor said, he did not care for. Money seemed to be of considerable importance to him. It was generally known that his wife browbeat him. Could he be bribed if the price were high enough?

He remembered Leslie Blake's furious words: "Do you think for one single moment that we'd rather have that than have him safely home?" But it was better not to think of Leslie, the miracle of her, with her loveliness, her warmth, her loyalty, her simple human kindness.

Easy to say but hard to do. That first meeting, her hand on his arm, her voice calling out with such gladness. Since then every encounter had made him more aware of the wonder of her. But—if she knew the truth about him? What then? Suppose he were to see in her eyes what he had seen in Jane Williams's: shock and disgust and fear? See her run from him.

Anyhow, she wasn't for him. According to her best friend, she was on the verge of marrying Oliver Harrison. Not Harrison, of all men! But there was nothing he could do to stop it, not if she loved the man, and women appeared to find him irresistible.

The evening was still warm and the sandy path along the river was white in the moonlight. The trees overhead rustled in a light breeze, sounding like soft rain. Shaw continued his walk at a long easy stride. Already he had regained almost all his normal strength and he enjoyed the exercise.

There was a light splash and he looked toward the river. A canoe went past him. Jim Mason was out for his evening drill. Instinctively Shaw stood motionless, close to the trunk of a big oak tree. It seemed to him that Mason was looking directly at him. Then he realized that the clerk had turned his head, that he was peering at the barge across the river, moored at the foot of the Blakes' lawn where it sloped to the river. What on earth was the man doing?

A paddle lifted, the canoe went on up the river and Shaw shrugged his shoulders. He looked at the luminous dial of his watch and turned back toward the covered bridge.

The usual group of women rocked on the porch of the Fox and Rabbit, chattering their heads off, sounding, he thought, like hens clucking in a barnyard. They broke off to watch him go up the steps, several of them calling "Good evening" as he went by. Lonely women, reaching out tentacles of words to hold a stranger in conversation, even for a moment.

The door to the lobby was open for coolness, and as he went inside he heard a woman's voice, raised indiscreetly, say, "Well, I guess he wasn't out with *her* tonight. She's still up in her room."

By *her* he gathered that the gossiping women were talking about Felice Allen. Several times she had imperiously beckoned him to her table and they had dined together. If he had been vain he would have believed she found him attractive, but he was detached enough to notice how shrewd and probing her questions were. Attracted or not, she was chiefly interested not in Donald Shaw but in his background. Much too interested, he thought uneasily, and he tried to arrange his dinner time so as to avoid her.

He unlocked the door of his room, switched on the light, and then stood motionless. After a long time he turned to close the door behind him.

Whoever had searched his room had done a thorough job. Every drawer had been taken out, emptied and turned upside down, in case anything had been fastened to the bottom. His bed was mussed as though someone had searched the springs and mattress. The pockets of his suits were inside out. His shoes had been moved.

"Well!" he said aloud. He grinned. "Well, it was a good try, anyhow." He locked the door, removed his right shoe and pulled out a folded paper. Sitting at the small desk, his face suddenly hard, he wrote a letter, enclosed the paper he had taken from his shoe, and addressed the envelope to the Gypton Company. It was marked: *Personal. Confidential.*

*   *   *

He mailed the letter at a box in the next village, some eight miles away, and left his motorcycle propped behind a rather dark and dismal-looking tavern with a battered and misleading sign, YE OLDE TRAVELERS' REST.

Inside it was as dark and dismal as on the exterior, with imitation oil lamps and bare tables in booths. At least, Shaw thought in satisfaction, there was no jukebox. In fact, there seemed to be no sign of human life.

Then a man rose from the last booth and peered out cautiously. Shaw went back to join him, and a waiter, who had come from behind the swinging doors to the kitchen, took their order.

"Well, Nors?" Shaw said. "Make out all right?"

"Sure," the guard told him. "I just asked to be relieved a coupla nights a week. After all, I've got thirty-five years of service behind me. Got a good man as a replacement."

"Can you count on him?"

"Think I'd have picked him if I hadn't been sure?" Nors Swensen pushed his rakish cap to a belligerent angle on his graying head.

Shaw grinned at him. "Okay, keep your shirt on. Anything new?"

Nors shook his head glumly. "But maybe things will pick up now. How about you?" The guard examined the tall man facing him. "You sure look better than the first time I saw you. Put on some weight, haven't you? Look like you could take on anyone your own size. And you don't act so darned grim. More like you are enjoying life."

"I'd hardly say that I am enjoying it, but at least it is interesting. I have a couple of items for you but I'm not sure what they add up to, if anything."

"Tell me," Nors said eagerly.

"My room at the Fox and Rabbit was searched sometime during my absence this evening. And I mean searched. Brother! Not a thing overlooked."

Nors's face stiffened. "They find anything?"

Shaw grinned reassuringly. "Nothing there to find. There never is."

There was no answering smile on Nors Swensen's rugged face. "But you've got notes somewhere."

"I carry them on me."

"Suppose you get knocked on the head some dark night. You ought to find somewhere else for safekeeping."

Shaw gave a low laugh. "Perhaps where I found the blue sheets of data Harrison wanted me to look for?"

Nors was not amused. "Someone is on to you," he said

stubbornly. "That's the only explanation. And it's no laughing matter."

"I don't see how anyone can be. Let's say that someone may be suspicious."

"I don't like it. You'd better look out for yourself."

Shaw laughed softly. "I intend to."

"Now who do you suppose—" Nors broke off as the door opened and footsteps sounded on the floor, a woman's high heels, a man's heavier tread.

"Heavens, it's dark in here," the woman said in a husky, low-pitched voice.

Shaw slid down in his seat so that his head was below the top of the booth partition. Nors raised his eyebrows. His lips shaped the word "Who?"

"At least there's no one else here," the man answered. "That's the main thing."

Shaw's gray eyes narrowed, his lips parted in sheer astonishment. The waiter hastened in from the back. The couple had taken the front booth. While they gave their orders, Shaw whispered, "Harrison and Miss Allen, that redhead at the Fox and Rabbit."

The waiter went out and the girl said, "What a hole-in-corner sort of place! You ought to have known better, Oliver, than to bring me to a place like this."

"Look here, Felice, you agreed to let me run things my own way."

"But—"

Harrison's voice rose. "That's the way they are going to be run. I know exactly what I am doing, and I won't tolerate any interference."

"My, my," she mocked him, "what a big boy you've turned out to be."

"Big enough to handle you and don't forget it. Now go back to New York, where you should have stayed all the time, and don't leave there again until I give the order."

"I'll go where I please and when I please," she said angrily. "I'll live my life just the way that suits me best."

"Exactly what do you think you are doing?" There was a snarl in Harrison's usually smooth voice. "I warn you, Felice, if you try to spoil things for me, I'll make you sorrier than you've ever been in your life."

"I was just checking up," she said sullenly.

"Checking up on what?"

"That's what I'm not sure of," she said slowly. "I just don't trust you, Oliver, my sweet. I don't trust you an inch. We had it all worked out but—"

"Well?"

"I think you're trying to change the program. Something has happened to you and I can't figure out what it is. If it's the Blake girl, I can tell you right now that you are wasting your time."

"Yes?"

Harrison's amused confidence made Shaw want to hit him, but he remained silent in the booth.

Felice Allen was not impressed. "Yes. You may be Clark Gable to the rest of the girls in that hick village but not to Leslie Blake. She's in love, all right, but not with you. I saw her face the night of the buffet supper. You can't miss it, that springtime beauty a girl gets when she falls in love for the first time." It was the bitterness of disillusioned experience in her voice rather than her words that carried conviction.

"Who is he?" Harrison demanded.

The girl did not answer. Then she gave a muffled cry. "Oliver, you're hurting me!"

Shaw started to get up but Nors's massive hand clamped on his arm, holding him down firmly.

"Who is he?" Harrison repeated savagely.

"Find out for yourself! But I'll tell you this. Double-cross me and you'll be sorry. Twist my arm all you like, but I mean it. And *he* means it. Don't underrate us. That's your weakness, my love. You always overrate yourself and underrate other people. You aren't going to play any tricks on us now and that is a plain warning."

"And just what does that mean?"

"If we don't cash in one way, we intend to do it another. Is that plain enough for you?"

"Blackmail! You wouldn't dare!"

"Try me," she said softly. "Just try me."

"I'd like to wring your neck," Harrison growled.

The door from the kitchen swung open and the waiter came out, balancing a tray. Knowing that she was safe in his presence, the girl laughed mockingly.

"Don't I know it! But watch your step, darling. Because, believe me, we are watching you."

"Check, please," Oliver said and flung down some money. "Come along."

"But I haven't even tasted—"

"Come along with me and come now or you can walk back to Claytonville by yourself. It's a good eight miles. I can see you doing it in those high heels." His words were like a whiplash.

The girl stood up, preceded him to the door. Before she went out she said, her voice rising deliberately, clearly, "At least, if they find me beaten up, they'll know where to look for the man who did it."

Oliver followed her out and the door slammed with a crash behind him.

The waiter whistled. "Whadda ya know? Wonder what made her say that?"

"Life insurance," Shaw said grimly.

The waiter laughed and then sobered. "Maybe. But I'd put my money on the lady. You shoulda seen her face. She don't have that red hair for nothing. I guess she can fight her own battles. Well, you see all kinds." He shrugged his shoulders and the swinging doors closed behind him.

"And what," Nors asked, "did you make of that?"

"I don't know," Shaw said thoughtfully, "except that there are storm signals out. Something is going to blow up in our faces if we aren't careful."

"We'll be careful," Nors said with stolid assurance. "Now, have you got anything else? We'd better separate before people start dropping in here for the evening."

"Only a man in a canoe."

"Are you kidding?"

"Not at all."

"A canoe? What was he up to?"

"That," Shaw admitted, "is what I have been trying to figure out."

xi

ON a Saturday morning, two weeks later, Leslie was working at her sculpture in her attic studio. She had been at it for three hours, with the radio turned to WQXR for the music. The notes of *Swan Lake* brought to her memory the lovely movements of that romantic ballet and she contrasted them, in their lyrical grace, with the figure that was taking shape on the armature.

No grace here. Only a living, striving body, pulling, clawing at the mountain. It was, she knew, the best thing she had ever done. If only she could finish it as she had conceived it. She had, little by little, lost sight of the festival. It was no longer her objective; only the sculpture itself absorbed her. There was a strength, a boldness of line unusual in the work of women sculptors, as though she had done something better than she knew.

She sat back, stretching her arms and her tired back.

"About time," Paul Logan said from the doorway, and she looked up in surprise. "Sorry. I didn't mean to startle you."

"Hello, Paul. I didn't hear you come in."

"I know. I've been here nearly five minutes; you were completely absorbed. May I see?"

"Well," she began reluctantly, "it's not finished, of course."

He came to stand behind her, looking at the figure with its face pressed against the cliff. Only the taut muscles of the back could be seen, the straining arms and legs. Paul made no comment at all.

Leslie got up to cover it with wet towels. "What do you think?" she asked at length, disturbed by his silence. Perhaps, after all, she had overestimated her work.

"I didn't say anything because praise from me would be impertinent," he said quietly.

Her face glowed. "Oh, Paul! You like it? You really think it's good?"

"Better than good. You must realize that yourself."

82

"I—hoped so."

He smiled suddenly. "Come on, Sobersides. It's a wonderful day. What is so rare as a day in June? The roses in the garden are all dressed in their prettiest colors for you. I thought we might swim off the barge for a while and then go to the Country Club for lunch. Doris and Jane are going to be there and I've invited that young doctor, Fletcher, the child specialist, who looked after Jack while he was ill. He has fallen for our Jane with a loud crash."

Paul added, rather uncertainly, "I brought along Shaw to even up the numbers. That motorcycle of his conked out for good and he has decided to buy a car but he won't have it until sometime next week. Suit you?"

"Fine," she agreed, her tone sounding careless.

"That's a relief," he said as though he meant it.

"Why?" she asked in surprise.

"Because Jane isn't going to like it one little bit. She's got a wild prejudice about Shaw and told Doris she didn't want him invited to Web Rock again. But for my money he's a nice guy, so I brought him along to join the party."

"You were right. Anyhow, Doris likes him."

"Yes. Well—"

As Paul hesitated, Leslie looked up in surprise, saw his expression. "Oh!" she said, enlightened.

Paul's color deepened. "Well," he explained rather defensively, "you've been busy with your sculpture and lots of other dates, as usual. Not that I shouldn't be used to that by now. So Doris and I got involved, as partners, in that tennis tournament, and I've been swimming at Web Rock and—what with one thing and another—you see how it is."

Leslie's eyes were dancing. "And—she's not a Sobersides."

He grinned ruefully, saw her expression and laughed outright in capitulation. "She's a little darling," he admitted. "We've been having a lot of fun together."

"I'm terribly glad."

"So Shaw goes along more or less as your partner. Is that okay?"

Leslie had started down the stairs ahead of him and she did not turn around. "Of course." She tried to keep the betraying gladness out of her voice. "You know where to change, don't you?"

"Sure. Too bad that Shaw doesn't swim, but he said he'd enjoy watching and waiting."

Leslie was annoyed to find her heart pounding as she ran across the lawn in a brief bathing suit, holding her cap in her hand, her soft curls giving off copper-colored lights in the bright sun. Donald Shaw, looking very tall in white slacks and jacket, was standing at the foot of the lawn, examining the barge.

"Hello, there," Leslie called. "Isn't this a miracle of a day, Mr. Shaw?"

He turned to face her. It seemed to Leslie that she had forgotten how strikingly good-looking he was. He smiled and took her outstretched hand. "A miracle," he agreed. "But does it have to be Mr. Shaw? Donald sounds more friendly. And Don is even better."

She lifted her eyes to his, saw his look, and was furious to realize that she was blushing.

"Donald to start with," she said with a laugh, "and I am—"

"Leslie. Yes, I know. According to Doris and Logan, you have practically gone into seclusion. We've been sent with firm orders to storm the citadel and rescue the princess."

Leslie laughed and drew a long breath of the scented air. "I'm so glad you did! Think of missing all this. How do you like our barge? According to family decree, it is a permanent part of the scenery. It was Douglas Clayton's playhouse when he was a boy and Dad is faithful to his trust."

Donald's smile faded. He turned back to his study of the barge. "So this was Douglas Clayton's sanctuary."

"Perhaps it still is," Leslie said.

He looked at her, a startled expression in the gray eyes that were usually so cool, so amused, so detached.

"Aunt Agatha," she explained, "said not long ago that Douglas Clayton seems to haunt this house, that he is more alive now than he ever was. So if he is haunting any place, it's bound to be the barge."

"Aren't you afraid of ghosts?" he said lightly.

"Not of his. Sure you won't change your mind and swim?"

He looked wistfully at the water. "I'd like to. It's a temptation. Perhaps another time?"

"Doctor's orders?"

"Something like that." He turned to look out at the river as some movement caught his eye. Jim Mason was going by in his canoe. The sun sparkled on the water, shone on his bare head with its sandy hair. Suddenly Donald's expression changed. His eyes narrowed, he watched the accountant intently.

"Now I wonder," he said.

Leslie laughed. "That's Jim Mason from the Company. Canoeing is his hobby. He practically patrols this part of the river, up as far as our house and down under the covered bridge below the Company."

"Does he indeed?" There was something odd in Donald's voice and in his manner. "Has he been with the Company for a long time?"

"No, you and he are the only newcomers to join us in months and months. The last one was Oliver Harrison, who has been here over ten months now. The rest have worked for the Claytons much longer; with some of them, their fathers and grandfathers and even great-grandfathers were part of the organization in one capacity or another."

"So," Donald said thoughtfully.

Paul ran down on the lawn, waved to them, jeered, "Sissies!" Then he climbed out on the barge and dived. Leslie followed him with a perfect swan dive. While they swam, calling to each other and laughing, Donald sat on the edge of the barge, watching. How beautiful Leslie was, her lovely body seen through the clear blue water like a mermaid's, arms that had been browned by the sun flashing now and then as she swam. Her face lit up with her smile like the sun coming from behind a cloud. He prayed that there would be no clouds for her, and yet, if Blake were to be proved guilty of taking a bribe, the storm would have to come and he would not, if he could, raise a hand to stop it.

He took a long breath. He'd rather lose an arm than hurt this lovely girl, cast a shadow on her life, but he could not turn back now. Anyhow, there was courage in her face, strength in her chin in spite of the softening effect of that bewitching dimple.

When Leslie and Paul had changed, all three crowded into the front seat of Paul's car and they drove to the Country Club. Under a big umbrella on the lawn a table for six had been reserved for them. Jane and Doris were already seated, with young Dr. Fletcher in attendance.

As they reached the table, Jane looked up and her face stiffened. She spoke to Leslie and Paul, but she did not even look at Donald Shaw as she greeted him with a minimum of enthusiasm.

"Hi, there," Doris called eagerly to Leslie. "I told Paul to bring you if he had to drag you by the hair and you screamed every step of the way."

"That's just what I did," Paul declared. "Didn't you hear the outcries? People in the village thought it was air raid sirens." He pulled out Leslie's chair.

"What on earth have you been doing to yourself?" Jane asked in surprise.

"Nothing special," Leslie said. "Working."

"A new hairdo?"

Leslie shook her head.

"Well, you're like another creature. Maybe it's that white dress. You're simply blossoming, whatever it is. And such a wonderful color you have."

Leslie felt her betraying color deepen. She looked up, saw Doris's swift look of understanding, looked down again. This is ridiculous, she thought. I'm wearing love like a flag for all to see, and he isn't even interested in me.

Doris, quick to protect Leslie, said, "Talking about being another creature, what's happened to your stepmother? Paul and I were at the Randalls' last night when she dropped in with your father. She was—I don't know—but not a single word about 'my own money.' She didn't try to—well, I mean she'd say things like 'What do you think, Corliss?' Or she'd say, 'It depends on what Corliss wants to do' or 'My husband makes decisions like that better than I do.' So—well, she was just different. Not helpless, exactly, but sort of gentle, as though she needed your father's protection."

"She has always been that way inside," Leslie said. "It has taken me a long time to understand her, much too long a time. She loves us, Dad especially, but she didn't know how to show it."

Jane, her serene beauty emphasized by the deep blue of her dress and a tiny blue hat perched far back on the smooth blond hair, was careful not to look at Donald Shaw. She was devoting herself to Dr. Fletcher, much to his satisfaction.

"This is too nice a party to break up," the doctor suggested. "Can't we all get in some tennis this afternoon and dine and dance here tonight? I'm a free man for the day and I want my holiday to be perfect. There's a new orchestra coming up from New York."

Jane gave him a languorous smile. "I'd love it."

Paul turned a stern look on Doris. "Speak your piece, wench."

"Yes, sir. At your beck and call, sir," she said meekly, while her black eyes sparkled.

Donald Shaw raised questioning brows. "Leslie? Will you?"

"That would be fun." She smiled at him.

*   *   *

That afternoon, on a bench beside the club court, Leslie, in white from bandeau to shoes, reveled in the beauty around her. Lovely world! Mauve, pink, jade and gold. Summer caught at one's breath like the far-away music of the bands of an approaching regiment and made one's heart jumpy.

Paul and Doris had beaten Donald and her at three sets of tennis. Warm, slightly tired, piqued by defeat, she was in a mood to steer her always temperamental ship straight for the rocks.

When Jane and Dr. Fletcher had replaced her and Donald on the court, she sat watching, with Donald curled up at her feet.

"Corking serve Jane has," he commented after a long silence, when he had watched Jane with brooding eyes.

"They're just letting her win," Leslie said, and gasped. What had made her say anything as contemptible as that? She was not only a bad sport; she was jealous, green-eyed with jealousy.

Unexpectedly, Donald looked up at her. "Don't be a little idiot." He smiled into her stormy eyes. He went on deliberately, "Jane is a superb tennis player, though she is getting a bit old for so strenuous a game. She is extremely beautiful." He added with cool detachment, "But that's all. Under that beauty—nothing, nothing whatever. No heart, no compassion, no understanding, no imagination. Any man who loved her would be very lonely, find his life very cold, unless he could be satisfied with an unrealized dream."

His hand reached up, touched hers. It was like an electric shock that ran through her veins. There was a tenderness under the laughter in his voice that shook her heart. "You're not really beautiful, you know, but you're like a hearth in winter, glowing and warm. You've got a temper, but you've also got a heart. You're—bewitching and enchanting and your moods change so no man will ever know what to expect next, and he's going to love every minute of it."

He stopped short. Leslie was staring down at him, at the short-cropped hair on which the sun beat relentlessly, and the scars, dozens of them, on his scalp. He looked up into the brown eyes that had widened. Then he got to his feet with a quick, lithe gesture.

"Let's forget it," he said harshly. "I'll be seeing you around, I suppose." He turned away.

She caught at his arm. "You'll be seeing me tonight," she said evenly. She knew now what had made Jane run away from him, knew the extent of the wound she had inflicted. "Remember? You asked me to dine and dance with you."

He lifted her hand to his lips. "It's still a date?"

"Still a date," she promised. She smiled impishly. "Just try to break it!"

It was a date that turned her eyes to stars while she dressed in orchid linen, as delicate as a handkerchief. Donald was waiting in the hall, talking with her father, when she came down the stairs. The older man looked from his new chemist to his radiant daughter with a troubled expression.

While she pinned on the orchids Donald had brought her, she laughed. "You must be a mind reader."

"Perhaps you ought to be, too," he said, with a glint of laughter in his eyes.

Blake put his hand on her shoulder. "Have fun, Puss. Good night, Shaw. Look after her."

"I will, sir."

They went to the dance in the village taxi, for which Donald apologized. He'd be able to do better next week.

"A white Chrysler?" Leslie asked mischievously.

"Well, no; a Volkswagen. But at least you won't have to ride in a sidecar."

"I like sidecars," she assured him blithely.

"I believe you do." He laughed as though at a hidden joke.

"What's wrong with that?" she demanded.

"Not a thing. I was just trying to imagine Jane in a sidecar."

"Oh."

The same three couples dined at a choice table on the edge of the dance floor. Tonight Doris seemed like a flame in the cranberry-red dress that had so intrigued her in New York. Though she had little share of Jane's beauty, she almost eclipsed her older sister by her sheer radiance. Happiness sparkled in her, made people turn to smile with sheer pleasure in her pleasure.

Doris herself was unaware of anyone but Paul Logan, who looked slightly dazed but enormously pleased with himself. Dr. Fletcher, plainly dazzled, devoted himself to Jane, seating her at the table as carefully as though she were made of crystal. Recalling Jane's strenuous tennis, Leslie smothered a laugh.

Crabmeat cocktail was followed by a clear soup, filet mignon with mushrooms, asparagus hollandaise, hot rolls and a tossed salad.

Jane groaned. "Heavens, I'll have to reduce for a week after this. I have no character when it comes to asparagus hollandaise."

"It's against nature to fight this sort of thing," Doris declared. "I may end as plump as a cantaloupe but it's going to be worth every pound. Paul, do you think they'd bring any more hot rolls?"

"Not for you," he said firmly. "I like my women slender."

She sighed, hesitated, and after a bitter struggle of all of one second, reached for the roll on his plate. She buttered it lavishly. "On mature consideration, I've decided that you'll have to take me as I am."

"I never thought I'd end by marrying a fat wife," he groaned.

"Fat! One hundred and twelve pounds," Doris protested.

"Marry!" Jane exclaimed.

Doris nodded. She nudged Paul. "Say something, you dope! Prove that you are the master of the occasion."

Paul stood up, grinning. "Ladies and gentlemen, permit me to announce my approaching marriage—"

"Doris," Leslie cried excitedly. "I'm so happy for you."

Paul frowned at her. "Now see what you've done, woman. You interrupted my speech. It was going to be terrific."

"When did this happen?" Jane demanded.

"This afternoon," Paul said. "I hit her over the head with a tennis racket and when she came to she wasn't able to fight back. She's mine now." He eyed Doris appraisingly. "A poor thing, but mine own."

The manager came up, beaming. In a bucket of ice there was a bottle of champagne. "We would like to extend our congratulations, Mr. Logan."

Adding to the spirit of the occasion, the new orchestra swung into the strains of "Here Comes the Bride," to the general laughter and applause of the guests, most of whom knew both Doris and Paul well.

Then the regular program of dance music began and Paul led a glowing Doris out on the floor, where again they were greeted with applause and laughter. Donald held out his hand to Leslie and swept her away among the dancing couples.

"Surprised?" he asked.

"I hoped it was going to happen. They're just right for each other. If any couple could be perfectly happy, except my father and mother, I think they'd be the ones. They want the same things out of life."

"Your parents are so happy?"

"Were," she corrected him. "Aunt Agatha is my step-mother. Dad told me my mother was like—like the sun shining on the Garden of Eden." They circled the floor in silence. "Sometimes I feel so sorry for Aunt Agatha. No woman can ever compete with a love like that, a whole, all-encompassing love, even when it is in the past."

Donald made no comment. Leslie was aware of Doris and Paul laughing together as they whirled past in one of the complicated new dances they liked to try out; of Jane looking up at the infatuated young doctor; of Felice Allen's red hair and husky laugh as she danced with Arthur Wilcox, one of Leslie's favorite people among the Company's employees. But they were all dreamlike. The important thing was the man who led her firmly, her steps following his as though they had always danced together. She looked up to see him watching her expression intently, with a somberness she had never before observed on the stern, handsome face.

"What's wrong?" she asked, missing a step as she was tumbled out of her dream.

He steadied her, moved on. "At least," he said, "you didn't run away."

She did not pretend to misunderstand him. At the moment his need mattered more than her own sickness of heart, her awareness that Jane was always there, always between them.

"You mean the scars on your scalp," she said steadily. "That's what Jane saw; that's what made her run away. You mustn't mind too much. She's—she can't help it, you know. She," Leslie added valiantly, "she is bound to get over it. Why, what difference do they make, after all? They are so tiny, practically invisible. They don't show except under a strong light. And, anyhow, there's nothing—disturbing about them. Nothing at all."

"Dr. Forsyth warned me, but I like sunlight and I keep forgetting."

"I'm glad you do." She looked up at him. "Something terrible happened to you, Donald. I don't know what. But you ought to forget it. Forever. After all, there's nothing left but scars."

He moved through the open doors onto the big screened porch that encircled the Country Club. "There's one other thing left. The sunlight. I won't be afraid of it any more."

He lifted her chin and kissed her lightly on the lips.

There was a sudden hush. The music had ended, and the scattering of applause. A woman stood in the doorway, a slender blond woman in white. Jane Williams. Then with a muffled exclamation—"No!"—she was gone and the porch began to fill up with couples, laughing and talking.

"Please take me home," Leslie said.

xii

NEXT morning Donald Shaw settled down at his desk in the Fox and Rabbit with a stack of paper in front of him. At an early hour he had had breakfast served in his room. By mid-morning he had filled pages with figures and formulas. The ringing of the telephone startled him.

"Shaw? This is Paul Logan."

"Oh, Logan. I didn't have a chance to congratulate you adequately last night. She's a delightful girl. You're a lucky man."

"You're telling me," Paul said exuberantly. "I can hardly believe my luck. How about joining me downstairs for brunch so I can let off steam by gloating for a while?"

"Thanks a lot, but I got an early start this morning. I'm a working man today. Give me a rain check, will you? We'll catch up on your gloating later."

Paul laughed, with the carelessness of a man who had never worked for his living and never expects to. "I hope they are giving you overtime. Dinner some night soon, then." He rang off and Donald went back to the paper before him, frowning at it. There was something he had missed.

Early in the afternoon the phone rang a second time. "Mr. Shaw, this is Agatha Blake. My husband and I hope you'll join us tonight for our buffet supper."

Again Donald excused himself. Most unfortunately, he had just made an engagement that he could not break.

"Next Sunday, then," she suggested and he accepted, wondering a little. Mrs. Blake had not impressed him as a woman who would issue a second invitation as soon as a first was refused.

When he had set down the telephone he stared at it, half tempted to call her back. Fool, he told himself, you could have seen her, talked to her. Leslie had been very quiet on the way home, had thanked him, said good night, and gone inside so quickly that he had been unprepared.

Leslie. He said the name aloud, thinking of the charming face with its warm brown eyes, small nose and resolute chin. He had not seen the dimple when she left him last night. That flashed only when she smiled and she had not smiled after Jane had turned away from the door, where she had witnessed the brief, fleeting kiss, when she had said "No" as though the word had been wrenched from her.

His thoughts switched from Leslie to Jane. For a long time he stared broodingly out of the window. He shook his head as though to rid himself of his thoughts, picked up his pen, put it down again. Jane. Her behavior had been odd lately, disturbingly odd. He wondered what was really going on behind those meltingly soft blue eyes. How he wished he knew! From the beginning she had been a risk, but a calculated risk. Sooner or later, she was quite capable of making trouble for him. He wished, as he had wished countless times, that he could guess from what direction the trouble would come, that he could be forewarned at least to some degree.

With determination he picked up the pen again and bent over his work.

The third call came, hours later, just as he was thinking of calling room service to order dinner. He heard a husky, enticing voice and recognized it at once.

"Hello, Elusive Stranger! This is Felice Allen, and bored to death. Won't you be an angel and dine with me? This village, more dead than alive, is driving me stark raving mad."

"I've wondered what its attraction could be for a dynamic girl like you, week after week," he confessed. There was a disconcerted silence at the end of the line and he grinned to himself. "That is awfully nice of you but I am tied up. The Blakes' buffet supper, you know."

"The time, the place, and the girl," she answered lightly. "Well, I can't say I blame you. There's all Agatha Winslow Blake's money as well as the Clayton money in the family, you know."

"So I've heard," he told her in a tone of detached amusement.

"I'll bet you have. Well, give me a ring sometime when you aren't engrossed in the Company." She slammed down the telephone.

He ate dinner in his room, in order to avoid seeing Felice, and then bent once more over the slim sheaf of papers, the result of the long day's work. Most of them he tore up in small bits, burning them patiently in his big ashtray and scattering the ashes. There was always the chance that his uninvited guest might pay another call. The three pages that remained he folded and slipped inside his shoe.

For a while he read a paperback copy of *Nicholas Nick-leby*, which he had picked up in the drugstore. He had not read Dickens since he was a boy and he sat chuckling over Mrs. Nickleby, Vincent Crummles, and the Infant Phenomenon. In a lot of ways, Dickens was still the greatest novelist of them all.

It was late when he put down the book, changed to dark slacks and sweater and let himself quietly out of his room. There were voices from the lobby of the Fox and Rabbit where a bridge game was in progress. He went softly along the hall, opened a side window, and climbed down the fire escape, grateful that it was out of sight of the street.

Once clear of the inn, Donald walked toward the covered bridge, switching on a flashlight to guide him through it. Before emerging, he turned it off and stood waiting for his eyes to adjust to the darkness.

He looked toward the Company buildings. Somewhere on the grounds a light flashed. Nors must be making the rounds. Then, in rapid succession, there was a loud crash followed by a shot; then silence, utter and complete.

Donald raced toward the sounds, hoping he would not stumble over anything in the dark but not daring to risk his flashlight. Around the corner of the laboratory, something like a dark shadow lay on the path, a long bundle of some sort. Donald struck it with his foot, tripped, and his arms flailed wildly while he regained his balance.

It was a body over which he had stumbled. His heart missed a beat as he switched on the light, saw the man in guard's uniform lying on his face, saw grizzled hair. He dropped to his knees, touched gently the lump on the guard's head, turned him over, felt the warm skin with a deep grunt of relief.

"Nors!"

The guard groaned, put up a groping hand to touch the lump on his head, opened his eyes. The man bending over him observed that the eyes were unfocused, that they did not see him.

"Lab—lights—woman hurt—shot—" His eyes closed again.

Donald looked at him in perplexity, reached for the keys Nors carried on a steel chain fastened to his belt. The belt and the keys were gone but the revolver was still in his hand. He had evidently fired a shot in warning.

He took the guard's hand and said slowly and clearly, "I'll take care of things. I'm coming back. Do you understand?"

There was no answer.

Donald picked up Nors's flashlight, which was more powerful than his own, and ran toward the laboratory. He tried to open the door but it was securely locked. He raced around to the back. His light caught a broken window. That accounted for the crash he had heard. Moving gingerly among the jagged pieces of glass, he climbed over the sill, flashed the light around.

On the floor a woman lay on her side, her cheek darkening from a heavy blow, blood streaming from a gash on her arm. Gently he cut away her sleeve with a penknife, staunched the bleeding with his handkerchief, then tied it firmly above the wound to stop the flow of blood.

A mop and pail were near her. She wore a neat housedress. A cleaning woman, but a superior sort of cleaning woman, Donald thought, as he saw the sensitive features. He groped for her pulse, found it. A feeble pulse, irregular.

Carefully he felt her legs and arms, but there seemed to be nothing broken. Nevertheless, he hesitated to move her in case of a possible back injury. It was easy to reconstruct what had happened. Someone had smashed the laboratory window to get in, had been surprised by the cleaning woman and had stabbed her with a knife and then knocked her out. Nors, hearing the noise, had come running, firing a warning shot. The man had evidently doubled back behind him, knocked him out and stolen his keys.

In the next room there was a creaking sound with which Donald had grown familiar. He sat up alertly. Someone had opened the supply cupboard whose creaking hinges were a joke among the chemists.

He stood up, moved quietly toward the door, knocked against the mop, which fell on the floor with a crash. Instantly the intruder in the next room flung open the door on the far side. With caution no longer necessary, Donald opened his own door, racing after the other man. By the time he had reached the far door of the laboratory, the heavy outside door opened, crashed shut. A moment later, a car motor roared, lights flashed on, and the car was gone before Donald could get outside. Without a car of his own, he had no way to follow.

He went back to the unconscious woman, bent over her again. Then someone leaped at him, clawing for his throat.

"What are you doing to her?"

With difficulty Donald shook him off, turned to face a young man who glared at him, ready to spring.

"Someone broke in, struck her and got away." Donald's voice was quiet. "The guard has been knocked out, too. Who are you?"

"Charles Turgen." The young man was on his knees now, lifting the woman gently in his arms. "She is my mother. Is she badly hurt?" There was agony in his voice.

"I don't know, but I don't believe I'd move her if I were you. The telephone in the next room is connected all night because we sometimes work late. Call the police and get me an ambulance."

The boy darted away. When he came back, he sank down on his heels, holding his mother's hand. "I'll kill the man who did this, who hurt her."

"Don't be a fool," Donald said sharply. "There has been enough violence here tonight."

"She—you don't know what she's like," the boy said, and Donald realized how young and vulnerable he was, scarcely out of his teens. "I've been going to law school at night, working my way through by handling a garage job during the day. Then that—that—" He swallowed. "Harrison got me fired because his new car was delivered to him without oil. Okay, so that was my fault. But I had an abscessed tooth that day and I was about crazy with pain and I couldn't take the time off to see a dentist. I got paid by the hour. I just plain forgot about the oil. Well, my mother said she'd make up the amount until I could land another job. This was all she could find, without training and all. She—she was doing this for me and she never even did any housework until my father lost everything because of a crooked partner. It killed him. But she said not to mind, that no honest work was degrading."

"She was right," Shaw said gently. "She's a fine person. So you want to be a lawyer."

"Not as a goal in itself. I want the training so I can qualify for the FBI."

"Then you had better learn to control that streak of violence, hadn't you?" The kindness in Donald's voice took away any offense. "The FBI is careful about the men it appoints." He raised his head. "That's a siren. If it's the ambulance, you're to go along with her. Tell the doctor he has my personal assurance that any needs of your mother will be met by me."

The boy got up. "How can I ever pay you back?"

Donald smiled. "You can help me, if you will."

"Anything," the boy said fervently.

"Then hop to it, and when she is all right, come back here. With the window smashed and the keys stolen, someone will have to be on guard all night."

The boy ran out and Donald stood looking down at the unconscious woman, thinking furiously. At least, he had acquired a devoted and loyal recruit, and at this point he could use one.

In a few moments the boy was back, followed by two white-clad young men with a stretcher. Gently they eased Mrs. Turgen onto it and lifted it.

"What about the guard?" Donald asked. "Have you seen him?"

One of the men laughed outright. "He must have a skull as solid as an oak tree. He's staggering but he's on his feet and ready to fight."

Donald grinned in relief as Nors came in. "Where's your car? We'll take you to the hospital as soon as young Turgen gets back to stand guard."

"You and who else?" Nors was fighting mad.

"What do you remember?"

"Well, I heard the crash when the window was smashed and I started to run. I fired off a warning shot. Then something landed on me like a ton of bricks and I went out." He gave a howl of rage as he made a new discovery. "My keys are gone!"

"Pipe down, I know they are. I've sent for the police."

"State police," Nors corrected. "Nothing here in the village but a constable. That woman—I could see through the window before I was slugged. Who is she?"

"A Mrs. Turgen, a cleaning woman who seems to have surprised the burglar. They've taken her to the hospital."

"Oh, yeah. I've noticed her around the last few weeks. A quiet, pleasant-spoken woman. Oh, there's another thing. Earlier in the evening I saw Mason out in his canoe, trying to look like Chief Sitting Bull."

"Mason again," Donald said thoughtfully. "He certainly keeps cropping up, doesn't he?"

"Well, it was no paddle hit me. It felt more like a sledge hammer."

Again a siren screamed in the night, rising and falling. Donald went to the front door of the laboratory to admit the state trooper. Behind him a car screeched to a halt, and Corliss Blake jumped out.

Donald told his story as quickly as he could, confirmed at every point by Nors Swensen. The trooper looked at Donald, at the dark slacks and sweater, at the tennis shoes, at the bloodstains on his arm where he had touched Mrs. Turgen.

"How did you happen to be so conveniently on the spot, Mr. Shaw?" he asked politely.

For once Donald hesitated, groping for a reply.

"I gave him a ring," Nors said unexpectedly. "I had a

feeling someone was prowling around and I figured it would take two of us to round up whoever it was."

"But why pick on Mr. Shaw?" The trooper's tone was unexceptionable but his bright eyes missed nothing.

Nors grinned. "He looked to me like the best bet if we were going to run into any kind of scrap."

"He sure does. I'd bet on him."

The men turned as Charlie Turgen came in. "I guess he saved my mother's life tonight by his prompt action. The doctor said the bleeding was stopped just in time. I owe Mr. Shaw a big debt." He looked at Donald a trifle anxiously. "They said she really ought to have a private room and blood transfusions. Is that all right?"

Donald nodded reassuringly.

Corliss Blake came back from the supply cupboard, which he had been investigating. "I think we all owe Mr. Shaw a debt. There wasn't time to steal anything. Your prompt action—" He broke off. "Let me give you a lift back to the Fox and Rabbit."

Donald shook his head. "Thanks very much, but you'd better take that stubborn Swede and haul him off to a doctor."

"Now look here," Nors began in protest.

"Can you arrange for someone to take over his duties for the night?" the trooper asked. "We can arrange for a man to patrol the plant regularly but we're short-handed."

Donald looked at young Turgen, who beamed. "You bet," he answered the unspoken question.

"Okay," Donald said. "Charlie and I will stay on guard for the night. One of us can board up that broken window and the other can do some patrolling. As long as the keys are missing we'll have to cover the whole place."

The trooper gave Donald a long look and turned to Corliss Blake for his decision.

"That's very good of you," Blake said heavily. "I appreciate this, Shaw. Come along, Swensen. I'll get you to a doctor."

"I've got to collect my revolver," Nors said. "Anyhow, I've always wanted to ride in a police car."

This time it was Donald who took a long suspicious look at the guard. The latter went out to the police car, careful not to meet his eyes, trying unsuccessfully to cover with his coat the bulge made by his revolver.

xiii

UP until the telephone call from the state police, the Blakes' buffet supper had followed its usual routine. The only exception had been the change in Oliver Harrison's attitude toward Leslie. From the moment when he first made his appearance, she had been aware of the difference in his manner. There had been a confidence in the carriage of his head, a determination that was excessive even for him.

As soon as the dancing started, he led her out on the terrace with a masterful air that alerted her. He held a chair for her and perched on the low stone wall, facing her.

"I'm worried about your father," he began abruptly. "This is strict confidence, of course, just between us. Something is going very wrong with the Company. In fact, it is just possible that unless drastic measures are taken, and taken immediately, there won't be any Company."

Leslie raised wide, startled eyes to his face. "As bad as that?" Her father's words were still fresh in her mind. This was confirmation of his worst fears.

"As bad as that," he told her grimly. "I don't know how much you understand about the new textile formula."

"Only what Dad said. That it is revolutionary and very important and—" She came to a halt. She had no intention of repeating her father's suspicions about Donald Shaw.

"You know that the Gypton Company has got onto it, and that they are getting information from someone in the Company?"

She nodded. "Dad told me they had made an offer for the formula that was—an insult."

"They did!" Oliver was jolted.

"Sorry," Leslie said, "I—thought you knew. That was strict confidence, too. I shouldn't have told you. But I just assumed—"

98

"That your father would keep me informed of developments." Oliver's tone was grim, tinged with resentment. "It was a natural assumption."

"Oliver," the girl said crisply, "I made a mistake and betrayed Dad's trust in me. But it was unintentional. I don't intend to discuss my father or his actions or his motives with you."

There was a frosty light in his eyes and then they warmed. "My darling, I'm afraid we're going to have to discuss the situation. You don't realize in the least what all this means."

"But—" she began in protest.

"It means," he said with deliberation, "that, unless something is done and done immediately, the Clayton Textile Company is headed for the rocks. That would involve the major part of the inhabitants of this village who draw their living from it. If that should happen, your father's position is going to be da—very difficult. The whole industry will blame him for the catastrophe because, as head of the Company, the final responsibility is his."

"But it's not his fault!"

"How much will that help him if he has to endure public disgrace?"

"Oliver!"

He reached down to take her shaking hands. "I know, my darling, how brutal this sounds. But we've got to face the facts, you and I."

"I don't understand," she choked, while her mind beat out the refrain: *Public disgrace, public disgrace, public disgrace.*

He drew her to her feet. "Your father is a nice guy, Leslie." Again there was an air of condescension in his tone that angered her. She tried to draw her hands away but his grasp on them tightened. "A very nice guy," he repeated. "But, let's face it, he is easy-going. Everyone likes him. He does his best. But—his best simply isn't good enough. He worked too many years as an individual; he hasn't the training, the thinking, of an organization man. He can't think big. He's not—well, not a natural-born leader. The time has come when a decision has to be made, when there must be a strong hand on the reins."

"And you have the strong hand," Leslie commented.

"I have the strong hand," Oliver assured her blandly. "Your father is just about ready to throw in the sponge, but if he loses the formula, he'll never live down the suspicions of people not only in the Company, not only in Claytonville, but throughout the whole industry."

"But what can be done?" Leslie asked, confused and frightened. "It would kill Dad to lose the respect of the Company, no matter how innocent he may be."

"There's only one way that I can see." Oliver slipped an arm around her. "I could find the man who is selling us out. I could save the Company. I could see that your father's reputation is safe."

Her face was radiant with relief. "Oh, Oliver!"

His arms tightened, drawing her close. "He is ready to retire, anyhow. If he does it now, if I become president of the Company, if you marry me, we'll fight this thing out together. We'll lick it. That's a promise."

Leslie's thoughts whirled. What Oliver said corroborated what her father had told her. Perhaps—if she could save him—protect him from dishonor, save the jobs of the people of Claytonville—perhaps personal happiness wasn't important.

Oliver, watching the conflicting thoughts pass over her face, laughed exultantly. He bent over, kissed her lips, long and deliberately.

Instinctively, Leslie pushed him back. She knew in a flash that, whatever the cost, this was one mistake she must not make. Even to save her father's reputation she could not marry Oliver Harrison. Every feeling rebelled.

"No," she whispered. "No!"

He laughed. He kissed her again. "My adorable Leslie."

"Let me go," she panted. "Let me go, I tell you." She was frantic to escape from his hands, his lips.

"Never."

"I'll scream for help."

His expression changed. His arms dropped. He looked at her in what appeared to be genuinely hurt surprise.

"What's wrong, darling? Don't be frightened. You'll learn to love me. I promise you will."

Leslie was surprised to hear herself say, "But what about your friend Felice Allen?"

Oliver's head jerked back in surprise. "Felice?" he repeated uncertainly. "Why? Are you jealous of her? I assure you, there's no reason to be."

Leslie laughed, a spontaneous ripple of mirth. Then it died on her lips as she saw the terrible look on his face. He knew from that lighthearted laughter that he had no hold on her at all, that he had lost her irrevocably. For a frozen moment they faced each other and Leslie discovered that she was afraid of this man. Then they became aware of the uproar, raised voices, exclamations of alarm from the sun room where the music had broken off abruptly.

Leslie turned away from him with a little shiver. "Something must have happened," she said. He followed her silently into the crowded room.

Corliss Blake's voice was raised, dominating the confusion. "Nonsense. There is no point in breaking up the party. The state troopers will have everything under control and they would probably prefer not to have too many of us milling around. Sorry I have to leave you. Good night."

He was gone before Leslie could speak to him. There was a babble of voices, talking excitedly, and Leslie made her way through the small groups of people, warding off the questions with which she was bombarded on all sides and to which she had no answer, hunting for Agatha.

The latter, looking placid and controlled except for the nervous twitching of her lips, was talking quietly to one of her guests. "I am sure," she said, "that Corliss would greatly prefer to have you stay here. Everything at the Company will be under control."

"What on earth happened?" Leslie asked. "Aunt Agatha, where has Dad gone?"

"The state police just called. Someone broke into the laboratory tonight. Swensen is injured. And some woman. The details weren't very clear. Your father has gone to see what the situation is."

Oliver gave a sharp exclamation. "A woman! There was a woman at the Company tonight?"

Leslie risked a look at him. Agatha's words had startled and angered him.

"Broke in!" he said after a moment. "My God, the formula—" He started for the door.

"Oliver," Agatha said in her placid voice.

He turned back impatiently. "Forgive me for rushing off but—"

"Oliver!" This time the voice was firm. "Corliss particularly requested that no one go over there. It will only cause confusion."

For a moment Leslie thought he was going to ignore her words. Then he turned back with a shrug of defeat. His lips were white with the effort he was making to control himself.

"Burglary," he said hoarsely. "If they've got away with it—" He broke off, his eyes roving around the room. "I don't remember seeing Shaw here tonight. Did he come?"

"I asked him," Agatha said. "He had another engagement."

"Shaw!" Oliver said thoughtfully. "From the very beginning, I've said—"

"Dear Oliver, I understand that you are greatly shaken.

None the less, you are breaking our house rules for a second time and I cannot permit it. Now will you be kind enough to ask the Company receptionist—Miss Morris, isn't it?—to dance? She is sitting alone in the sun room."

Oliver bowed slightly and went into the other room. With a look at Agatha, Leslie went in search of a partner, managed —for hours, it seemed—to carry on gay talk that had nothing to do with the burglary.

At last, Ann, the older of the two maids, came into the room, caught Agatha's eye. "It's Mr. Blake on the telephone."

For once Agatha moved swiftly, almost lightly toward the telephone in the library. With a murmured excuse to her partner, Leslie followed. Oliver, who apparently had been equally alert, was close behind.

"Yes, Corliss? . . . They got away . . . Then there was no harm done . . . Nors Swensen knocked out . . . a woman? . . . the cleaning woman seriously injured. Oh, dear! . . . smashed a window. Well, my dear, it might have been worse. When will you be home? . . . Good. But how about a guard? Can the police . . . Oh, Mr. Shaw was there. He'll stay on guard all night. I must say, that's very nice of him."

She set down the telephone, looked at Leslie. "You heard?"

Leslie nodded, her fingers groped for the back of a chair. She needed support.

Agatha looked at her stepdaughter and there was keen penetration in her eyes. "It's just as well," she said slowly, "that Mr. Shaw refused my invitation for tonight. He appears to be making himself very useful. Sit down, my dear. Oliver, bring her a glass of water, will you? Our guests are leaving. I'll take care of them, Leslie, so you just go straight to bed. I'm afraid—the heat—has been too much for you."

*   *   *

"I'm afraid the heat has been too much for you."

It was the following morning. Leslie was on her knees in the cutting garden, a trowel in her hand. The moist earth had a healing quality that dulled the pain in her heart. The early morning air was cool. She raised her eyes, seeking the cardinal whose sharp, clear, repeated call she heard. She saw a flash of flame against the blue of the sky. If only she could create something as lovely as the flight of a bird, leave behind her some record of the beauty she so loved.

She left the trowel thrust into the earth, the restlessness that had driven her out of doors before the rest of the household was awake having drained away. For the first time in her healthy young life she felt bone-weary, drained of energy, while listlessness made her droop.

"I'm afraid the heat has been too much for you."

She turned with a start, aware that she had heard the words before but that they had not registered clearly in the turmoil of her thoughts.

"Sorry, Aunt Agatha, I—" She looked up into the older woman's face, saw her concern, tried to smile.

"It isn't the heat," she confessed.

"I know." Agatha brought a garden chair near the flower bed and sat down.

Leslie moved to curl up at her stepmother's feet, her hands clasping her knees. "Because I nearly fainted last night?"

"Partly that. But I guessed long ago, the first time he ever came here. That's why I asked him to supper last night. I wanted to have a chance to—study him a bit. Not," Agatha added quickly, "that I had the slightest intention of interfering."

"There's nothing to interfere with," Leslie said dully. "Sometimes I think he cares for me; but there's Jane, of course."

"Jane Williams?" Agatha said in surprise. "Why I thought —" She hesitated. "Mr. Shaw has been seen dining frequently with Miss Allen at the Fox and Rabbit. You know how these things get around in a village. I thought she was the one." She put out her large, shapely hand. "Sorry, Leslie. Forgive me if you can. I'm a blundering fool. Somehow I always manage to say the wrong thing."

Leslie managed an uncertain, rather wavering smile. "It's all right. If Donald Shaw cares more for someone else, I'm not going to let it matter. Not for long, at any rate. I'll get over it. But he wasn't the burglar last night. He wasn't. He couldn't be."

"You are too honest to try to fool yourself or to fail to face the facts, Leslie. He refused my invitation because he claimed to have another engagement. But he seems to have been at the laboratory when Nors Swensen and a new cleaning woman, a Mrs. Turgen, were both attacked."

Leslie watched a butterfly with orange stripes flutter from flower to flower. "What does Dad think?"

Agatha made an oddly protective gesture toward Leslie and then met squarely the demand for truth in the girl's level eyes.

"Corliss doesn't know what to think," she admitted. "But he believes there was something queer—about the whole operation. Something staged. It was so noisy, to begin with. Nothing was stolen. And then the attack on Swensen and particularly the one on that poor cleaning woman were needlessly brutal. Corliss thinks the purpose of the whole thing was to indicate that it was an outside job, to clear any employee of the Company of complicity in case suspicion should be aroused."

Leslie reached for what scanty comfort she could find. "But Dad left—Donald—on guard for the night. He must have trusted him."

"There was no risk that anything would be stolen then. It would point too clearly at Mr. Shaw. At least, that's what Corliss thinks. The purpose had already been achieved. The presence of an outsider had been established."

Agatha got up heavily. "Don't forget that Jane and Doris are coming to lunch. They are the only members of the Committee I'm sure of, at this point, though I've telephoned like mad. But I've ordered a flexible menu in case any more of them show up."

"Committee?" Leslie said blankly.

"The Planning Committee for the Clayton Festival. There are so many members that no one has been taking any responsibility. You know how committees are as a rule. One person does all the work, the rest talk and feel important."

"Don't I know," Leslie said fervently. "The trouble with this town is that there aren't enough busy women. They are the ones who get things done."

"So," Agatha told her, "I'm going ahead more or less on my own. Corliss would be upset if this should fail—too."

Leslie took a long breath. "Nothing has failed yet, Aunt Agatha. We've got that to hang on to. Who was it who said, 'A lost battle is a battle you think you have lost'? We've just begun to fight."

She scrambled to her feet, gave Agatha a quick hug. "Bring on your Committee. We're going to make Clayton-ville sit up and take notice."

IT was a brave challenge, but when Leslie reached the lunch table, wearing a silky-looking cotton dress of browns and yellows, which reflected the brown tones of her hair and eyes and tanned skin, her enthusiasm began to dwindle. Three more members of the Planning Committee had appeared, all rather fretful and abused at having had to change their plans at the last moment.

Agatha fought a valiant but losing battle to get the women to cope with the program for the Festival. Mrs. Ballard had been having servant problems; Mrs. Hastings seemed to cherish the vague idea that the purpose of the Committee was to organize summer sports for youngsters; and Miss Eustace, a formidable woman with a bass voice, had come prepared with all her recollections of the Clayton family and its history, which included data that went back to the late 1600s.

Leslie, listening with dismay to the babble of voices, realized that it was less like conversation than a series of determined monologues.

Agatha: "We must start by drawing up a general plan. Then we can get down to the details, allot the work and do the minor things like deciding what kind of supper is to be prepared."

Mrs. Ballard: "Just what I told my Sarah this morning. 'If you'd make a general plan,' I said, 'you'd get your work done in half the time and twice as efficiently.' It's two weeks at least since any of the silver has been polished."

Doris: "So if we're to be married in August, I'll have to go to New York right away to pick out my trousseau."

Mrs. Hastings: "I think it would be nice to plan some picnics with someone to arrange races; you know, with potatoes or those three-legged ones, or something like that. So amusing. Children love them."

Jane: "Children love anything that is noisy and exciting,

and the noisier the better. Now Jack has persuaded one of the Company clerks to take him out in his canoe. But, if you ask me, Jim Mason is doing it only—"

Miss Eustace, her deep voice drowning out the others: "Of course, the Claytons were the first settlers here. Somewhere I've got some notes my mother made about the family. Very nicely written, too. It might be a good idea to have them printed and distributed at the Festival. Historical interest, of course. My dear mother made a hobby of genealogy, you know."

Everyone knew. Their hearts sank. Agatha gave Leslie an appealing look. Leslie finished her dessert of lime ice with melon balls and stood up.

"We must start planning now," she said crisply. "If we aren't going to make a disgraceful failure of the Clayton Festival, we've got to think hard and work hard. We owe Douglas Clayton a great debt. Let's put aside personal things and arrange to pay him the finest tribute we can." She looked from face to face, collecting their attention, forcing them to put aside temporarily their private concerns in the general interest.

"Now then, Aunt Agatha."

"First," Agatha Blake said, "we'll have a parade, of course. With three bands. Then the speeches on the Green and the unveiling of the sculpture. Finally, a supper in the Town Hall followed by a showing of the movie of the Tower Heights offensive. Now suppose we begin."

The Committee, considerably to its own surprise, settled down to work.

*   *   *

Late that afternoon, Agatha got out her cream-colored Buick and drove Leslie to the hospital. She drove easily and competently. Beside her Leslie suddenly burst into delighted laughter.

"When I think how you made them hew to the line," she chortled. "I didn't know you had it in you."

Agatha shared her laughter. "I've never fancied myself in the role of Madam Chairman but someone had to do something."

"Do you really think they'll do all they promised to do?"

There was a quirk of amusement on Agatha's lips. "Want to bet?" she asked mischievously.

Leslie laughed again. "Not I! You've not only got them eating out of your hand but they love it. They were terribly impressed by your efficiency and everyone wants to show you how much she can accomplish."

Agatha beamed. "I never realized before how interesting it is to find out what potentialities various people have. The only trouble is that it's a two-edged sword. Before I knew it, I began to get involved in all sorts of things. I found I had committed myself to taking part in everything from the PTA to civil defense."

"You're going to be knee-deep in village affairs before you are through," Leslie predicted.

"I expect I shall," Agatha answered happily. A flush on her cheeks made her seem younger, prettier, less stately and more approachable than usual.

She parked in the wide space reserved for visitors to the hospital. The receptionist smiled at them. "Good afternoon, Mrs. Blake. Hello there, Miss Blake. I hear there's been a lot of excitement going on."

"May we see Mrs. Turgen?"

The receptionist spoke over the telephone, shook her head. "Sorry, she's sleeping right now. But her boy Charles is in the sun room on the second floor, waiting for her to wake up. Perhaps you'd like to talk to him."

Agatha nodded. "We'll go right up. Now, about her expenses—"

"Charles Turgen told us that they are being taken care of by a Mr. Donald Shaw. Mr. Shaw telephoned to confirm that."

"That was very kind of Mr. Shaw," Agatha said, "but Mrs. Turgen is our responsibility. I'll appreciate having you bill me direct." Her tone was pleasant but the order was meant to be obeyed, and the receptionist made a note of it.

"And how is Nors Swensen getting along?"

The receptionist called again and hung up smiling. "They x-rayed his head. There's no serious injury. He is sitting in the sun room with young Mr. Turgen right now and he is to be released in the morning. Your husband has already called and left instructions that Mr. Swensen is not to report for duty for at least another week."

They took the self-service elevator to the second floor. Agatha was thoughtful. As the door opened she said in an absent tone, as though thinking aloud, "Conscience money."

Leslie made no comment. It was easy enough to follow the direction of her stepmother's thinking.

There were only four ambulatory patients in the sun room.

One was looking out on a street of arching elms, a second listened to a radio whose volume was tuned low, a third turned the pages of an illustrated magazine. The fourth, with a bandage like a turban wrapped around his grizzled head, was talking cheerfully to a slight young man with a worried face.

Leslie went to them with outstretched hand. "Hello, Mr. Swensen. That's very impressive-looking headgear you are wearing. Very becoming, too. No, don't get up, please, or we won't stay."

Nors settled back with a grunt. "This is nice of you, Miss Blake. Mrs. Blake, this is Charlie Turgen, whose mother got bunged up. He is waiting for her to be able to talk to him."

Agatha shook hands with both of them. "I'm so sorry about your mother's injury," she told Charlie.

His face hardened. "To knock her out was bad enough. I suppose the rat was afraid she would recognize him. But to slash her with a knife! There was no sense in that. She couldn't have done him any harm, even if she had wanted to. If it hadn't been for Mr. Shaw, she might have bled to death. He made a tourniquet and—"

"And lost the burglar," Agatha said quietly. "Not, of course, that we'd have had it any other way. If Mr. Shaw had tried to stop him, your poor mother might have been worse off. We are all grateful that he made the choice he did."

Nors gave her a quick look and shifted his position uneasily. To Leslie, who was watching him, there was an odd expression on his face, almost a look of guilt. She must be imagining things. The Swedish guard was one of the employees with the longest record of service in the Company and his reputation was untarnished. Still, it was queer that the person who had attacked Mrs. Turgen so brutally had inflicted little damage on Nors Swensen.

"Didn't you see the man who attacked you at all?" she asked. "Not even a glimpse?"

Nors shook his head and then grunted as though the movement had hurt him. "I heard the window crash when it was broken, and I started to run. I saw a woman lying in the laboratory on the floor and fired a shot. Then—I might as well have had the walls of Jericho fall on me. I don't remember another thing."

"I suppose the burglar took your revolver," Leslie said idly.

"He got my keys. That was bad enough."

"But he left you armed? How incredible. Especially when he took the time to rob you of your keys."

Nors shifted his feet again. He got up. "Well, I guess I've gotta get back to bed. Nice of you to come. I sure appreciate it." Small eyes made a quick, almost furtive survey of Leslie's face. "Queer things happen when people get excited, you know."

"Very queer," she agreed.

A nurse came to the door of the sun room, smiled reassuringly at Charlie Turgen. "Your mother is awake now and asking for you. But don't stay more than ten minutes, and don't excite her."

Out in the sunshine, Leslie took a deep breath of air that was sweet and free of the odors of ether and medications. She got into the car. Agatha turned the key in the switch, released the hand brake. Then she spoke abruptly. "No, Leslie, you must not do it."

"Do what?"

"Try to transfer the guilt, to find—someone else who struck down those two people."

"Just the same," Leslie said stubbornly, though she flushed a little at Agatha's insight, "Nors Swensen isn't telling the truth. That's why he was so eager to get away from us."

* * *

". . . and so," Charlie Turgen concluded, "she's going to be hospitalized for at least two more weeks and she won't be able to do any more heavy cleaning. And they told me, at the desk at the hospital, that Mrs. Corliss Blake insisted on taking over Mother's expenses."

"She did?" Donald grinned at the younger man. "Good. Then that makes it possible for me to put you on my payroll for a while."

"But, Mr. Shaw—"

"*Private* payroll," Donald told him. "Let's call it an apprenticeship for the FBI."

Charlie's eyes gleamed. "Are you going to figure this out for yourself?"

"No, *we* are, you and I. At least, we'll make a darned good stab at it." Donald added warningly, "But we must have one thing clear to start with. I know how you feel about the man who stabbed your mother and knocked her out. But that 'eye for an eye' theory has always struck me as sheer savagery, barbaric. Revenge is an ugly thing. An endless chain. The kind of thing that keeps family feuds continuing generation after generation. I get even with you, then you with me, then I—There has been enough violence. Whatever you learn or guess, discuss it with me before you take any action on your own. I don't want you to go off half cocked."

"I give you my word," Charlie said. "What do you want me to do?"

"I want some information. Find out all you can about the background of five people: Felice Allen, Oliver Harrison, Jim Mason, Corliss Blake, and Nors Swensen."

"How do you want me to go about it?"

Donald smiled at him. "Probably the finest government agency, not only in this country but anywhere in the whole world, is the group known as the American Postal Inspectors. Their record is unparalleled. We talk about the Canadian Mounties getting their man. But they can't touch the record of our own Postal Inspectors. Every single man works on his own plans and carries them out. He takes full responsibility for what he does. That's what I want you to do."

"I'll give it all I've got," Charlie promised.

"I know you will." Donald, who had been walking in the new picnic grounds with young Turgen while the Company employees were still at lunch, paused to light a cigarette. "Charlie, has anything struck you about that business last night, anything that seemed out of line?"

"Yes, sir," Charlie answered promptly. "It looks to me like an inside job masquerading as an outside one."

"That's just what I thought." Donald looked at Charlie. "What's wrong?"

Charlie smiled sheepishly. "I guess you'll think I am hipped on the subject because I hate Harrison for what he did to me, making me lose my job and all. But, well, darn it, he's the one guy I'm sure can be counted out. He was at the Blake buffet supper last night, with about twenty people to witness the fact. He has a perfect alibi."

Donald laughed at the younger man's chagrined expression. "You've got to keep yourself free of prejudice. It's facts we need. Solid, substantial, reliable facts. And nice concrete evidence to support them. Emotion should play no part in any investigation. Remember this, Charlie—angry people don't think."

"Okay," Charlie agreed. "When do you want me to get started?"

"Now, if you can. There's no time to waste." He opened his billfold. "Your first week's salary and expenses. If you need more, let me know. And keep in close touch." He looked at his watch. "Time I got on the job. Good luck to you."

When Donald entered the laboratory, he found it deserted except for a locksmith busily at work changing locks. Then Arthur Wilcox, Donald's favorite among the young chemists, returned from lunch.

"Hi there, Shaw. I hear you were on guard all night. You're a glutton for punishment. I didn't expect you to turn up today."

"I caught up on my sleep this morning," Donald told him.

"Just my luck," Wilcox grumbled good-humoredly. "I missed all the excitement. They tell me there was a lot of wild talk at the Blakes' buffet when they heard about the burglary, but I turned the party down—like a fool."

Something in Wilcox's tone made Donald's brows arch in a question.

Wilcox's pleasant face was embarrassed. "I got a telephone call at the last minute from that redhead at the inn. I'd had one date with her, took her to a Country Club dance. After all," he added defensively, "she is darned attractive."

"She is, indeed."

"But there is something about her—too much a hothouse plant for me. I decided to let her strictly alone. I've found the girl I want to marry and I'll try to talk her into it as soon as I get a raise. But last night Felice called me, asked me to have dinner with her at the inn."

Donald was about to say that he, too, had had a call from Felice. He decided not to. For all his deprecation, Wilcox was rather proud of his conquest.

"She has a way with her," Wilcox confessed. "But for all the flattery she dishes out, I got the idea she wasn't interested in me; it was the Company. And there she was too darned interested. She asked questions about Corliss Blake and Harrison and you and the formula. She didn't get any change out of me. When she realized that I had clammed up, she developed a sudden headache, so I left."

The laboratory phone rang and Wilcox scooped it up. "Yes, sir," he said. He turned to Donald. "Mr. Blake has called a general meeting in the restaurant. Only place big enough to hold all the employees. Right away."

By the time the two men entered the restaurant, the tables had been hastily removed and chairs had been placed in rows. In front, facing the rows of chairs, Corliss Blake sat on a small raised platform where, as Santa Claus at

Christmas time, he distributed presents to the children of the employees. He looked strained, haggard, as though he had aged overnight.

The employees filed into the seats as they arrived, without regard for their position. So it happened that Harrison, as a latecomer, took a seat behind the two chemists. They heard him mutter to the man beside him, "Blake can't handle this job. He ought to be forced to resign, if he can't see it for himself."

Then Harrison caught sight of Donald. He leaned forward. "I understand that you were Johnny-on-the-spot last night, Shaw."

"That's right," Donald told him cheerfully.

"I hope you are prepared to produce a lot of convincing explanations. The police are simple souls, you know. They are apt to jump at the obvious solution every time, and that is usually the man who just happens to be on the spot."

Wilcox gave Donald a startled look, started to speak, changed his mind.

The employees were all in the room now, but still Blake waited. There was a long uneasy pause and then the door opened and the lieutenant from the state police walked briskly up to the platform, trim in his uniform, and took the vacant chair beside Blake.

Donald grinned to himself. Anything less simple than the state police lieutenant he was unlikely to find, a quiet man with shrewd eyes, a determined mouth, and a look of great intelligence.

For a few moments the two men conferred in low tones. Then Corliss Blake rapped for order.

"Last night," he began heavily, "as most of you have heard by now, someone broke into the laboratory, apparently in an attempt to steal Formula GR. That attempt was unsuccessful because of the quick action of Mr. Shaw. But Nors Swensen, our night guard, was knocked out; Mrs. Turgen, a cleaning woman, was not only knocked out but ruthlessly stabbed, and while her condition is not critical it is serious."

He paused for a moment. "You have doubtless noticed that we have had a locksmith here this morning providing new locks, as Swensen's keys were taken from him after he was knocked out."

Again he paused. "Unfortunately, last night a series of problems came up that prevented the state police from making a prompt investigation; there were several bad multiple car accidents and a bank robbery that entailed setting up roadblocks. However, they are now at work, fingerprint men, photographers, and so forth, in the laboratory. The chemists will please not return there until the men have finished. But, as Mr. Shaw kindly stood guard last night, and someone has kept an eye on the laboratory all morning, there has been no opportunity to tamper with any evidence that may have been left on the scene."

There was a collective gasp. For the first time the personnel saw clearly that Blake and the state police believed the attempted burglary had been an inside job. There was an excited murmur.

Blake raised his hand for silence. "In the past, this has been a united, happy and loyal organization. Today, I appeal to you for that loyalty and for your support. If any of you has any information that would be helpful in the investigation, however slight it may seem to be, you can reach me at my house tonight. What you tell me will be held in the strictest confidence." He paused again. "I know I need not ask you to give Lieutenant Varelli your fullest cooperation." He looked at the lieutenant.

The latter stood up and spoke pleasantly. "I would like each of you, as you leave the restaurant, to permit the trooper who is waiting there to take your fingerprints." He smiled. "It is a very painless operation. Later, we will undoubtedly have to question some of you, perhaps a number of you. Please remain available." He started down the length of the room.

"Just a minute," Harrison said. "Has anyone found out how Shaw happened to be so opportunely on the spot last night? It seems to me that there is not much point in searching the laboratory. He had all night to clear away any incriminating evidence."

Donald was on his feet. Wilcox grabbed his sleeve. "Don't start a row," he begged him.

Across the room Donald could see Blake's eyes raking his face. He turned to the lieutenant, holding himself rigidly under control. "Whenever you want to question me—" he began.

"That's fine, Mr. Shaw," the lieutenant said politely. "Suppose you come along now."

Corliss Blake watched the two tall men walk out of the room. "The meeting is adjourned," he said heavily.

FOR July the weather was almost perfect, with sparkling air and a cool breeze that rustled the leaves, making them sound like light rain. Even in the attic studio there was a fresh breeze.

Leslie looked up as she heard Agatha's firm tread on the stairs. Never before had Agatha come up here. With all her well-meant interference in the past, she had always respected her stepdaughter's privacy.

"Good heavens!" Agatha exclaimed. "I had no idea it was so big."

"I realized I really had material for a bas-relief," Leslie explained. "I'm going to have it cast in bronze."

Agatha came slowly up to the massive sculpture. For a long time she looked at it. Then she turned to Leslie. "And I tried to discourage you! I didn't know—I didn't dream you had this in you. It's superb, Leslie!"

The girl who had looked increasingly pale and drawn as the days dragged by suddenly glowed.

"You have great talent, my dear; a gift that you must not neglect. And I am so terribly glad you have it. Perhaps if you were to go back to New York or even to Paris or Rome for more study—"

"I'll keep on sculpting," Leslie promised her. "But, somehow, I think this is the best thing I'll ever do. It seemed to shape itself, to progress like lightning."

"But you've worked hours every day," Agatha reminded her. "You've been shut up here without any relaxation or parties. Just a quick dip off the barge before dinner. You look to me as though you had lost pounds and pounds, and your tan has faded out. By this time of year you are usually as brown as a nut."

Leslie smiled at the anxious woman. "I had to do something or go stark crazy and I don't know any better way than to be completely immersed in hard work. And I couldn't

114

go out on dates, Aunt Agatha. I just couldn't. Everywhere I went I'd hear the same questions about the Company and the burglary, the same innuendoes about Dad and—Donald."

Agatha Blake smiled faintly. "Actually, you have done some needless worrying, child. I haven't shut myself off; I've kept the Planning Committee working at top speed for the festival and—not one single person has dared to say a word or ask a question."

"You're wonderful!"

"Nors Swensen has gone back to work and I've sent Mrs. Turgen to the Edgeworth for a couple of weeks of rest. She didn't want to do it but her son persuaded her. The most difficult part was providing her with a suitable wardrobe. I really had to be very firm about it."

Leslie smiled at Agatha's tone.

"She's a nice person, Leslie, well educated, cultivated. I've been hunting around in my mind, trying to think of some pleasanter way for her to earn her living, something that is less taxing on her health and her strength than house-work, something more congenial."

"But there are so few possibilities, so few choices in a village of this size."

"That's true, of course, but you know I bought the old Wentworth place on the Green, the stone house with ivy growing over it. There wasn't any need for it, but when I learned a garage was going up there that would ruin the character of the Green, I decided to save it. I'm going to give the village a library. Not now, of course, because there are people who might think the Blakes were trying to buy their good will. But when all the trouble at the Company is cleared up, I have an idea that Mrs. Turgen would enjoy being a librarian. In so small a place she wouldn't need special training, at least to start with, and I could help her get some courses at the University later on."

Leslie hugged her. "You're marvelous! You've carried on all alone and I've let you down terribly."

"Not at all." Agatha looked at the bas-relief. "This is the most important thing you could have done. Anyhow," there was an amused quirk to her lips, "I didn't really need any help." She looked back at the piece of sculpture. "But what happens to it now?"

"I'm taking it into New York to have it cast. Doris is having some fittings for her trousseau and Jane has an errand of some sort. She is being very mysterious about it. So we're going in her Cadillac. We can put this on the back seat. Just as well, because my little Renault would never have held it. But I'll need Hermann's help in getting it downstairs."

* * *

The gardener carried the clay bas-relief, swathed in cloths and heavily packed in newspapers, and laid it carefully on the back seat of the Cadillac.

"Good heavens!" Jane exclaimed. "It's as big as the town clock."

The three girls sat on the front seat. Jane was dressed in pale gold from hat to shoes and beautiful enough, Leslie thought with a pang, to stop traffic. But the big blue eyes seemed cold as glass. The beautifully shaped mouth had a curiously hard look. There was a tension about her that was unusual in a girl whose normal quality was a relaxed languor. She seemed to withdraw from her companions, to be intent only on her own thoughts.

Doris, in a blue sheath, spots of color burning in her cheeks, was busy making lists and muttering to herself: "Bridesmaids' dresses. Shoes. At least two new pieces of luggage. Warm coat. We're going to Scotland first, you know. Decorations for the church. Check the list of invitations. A dozen pairs of—heavens, how can I do it all in a month?"

"I'll help," Leslie promised. "And Jane, of course."

"You know," Jane suggested, "it might be smart to consult Miss Allen. She would have wonderful ideas and I'd be glad to pay her bill for consultation."

"Not that woman!" Doris protested. "I can't stand her. She makes me think of that line of Bacon's we studied in school: 'The cat knows whose lips she licks.' I'd dress in sackcloth and ashes before I asked her for advice."

"Why not try Aunt Agatha," Leslie suggested. "You'd be surprised to see how efficient she is. The more she has to do, the more time she seems to have at her disposal, like most busy people. And she'd love to have you consult her."

"You've changed your mind about your stepmother, haven't you?" Doris emerged for a moment from her lists like a flying fish, plopped down again.

"I never really knew her until all the—trouble started. She has been wonderful. No advice. No criticism. She keeps backing Dad, building his confidence, keeping the house a place of peace and refuge after the strain of the situation at the Company. She's like a tiger if anyone bothers him."

"They've never really found out anything more about the burglary, have they?" Jane said abruptly.

"They are working on it."

"Everyone in the village thinks it was an inside job."

"Now, Jane," Doris protested, "we aren't going to discuss it today."

"No one wants to discuss it at any time, so far as I can make out," Jane said coolly. "But it's not fair to the village or the Company to hush things up. It's all right for you, Leslie, making a statue, or whatever it is, of Douglas Clayton. It's all right for the Blakes to plan the Clayton Festival. But it was Doug's company, after all, and I am the woman he loved. I intend to do something more for his memory than cover up whatever is happening."

"What do you mean by that?" Leslie asked, her voice a tense whisper.

Jane pulled up the car in front of the building where the caster had his studio. "I've never trusted Donald Shaw. I'm going to find out the truth about him."

"Jane!"

"You're in love with him, Leslie. I saw him kissing you. I saw your face. Way off the deep end and stars in your eyes. But there is something wrong with that man and I mean to prove it, to expose him publicly."

"But why?"

"Because," Jane said, "that man is an impostor."

*   *   *

With Doris's help, Leslie got the sculpture out of the back seat.

"I'll meet you girls at the Plaza at five," Jane said. "Doris should have finished her fittings by then."

"Jane," Leslie said desperately, "where are you going?"

"You aren't going to stop me."

"I wouldn't dream of trying," Leslie said in blank surprise.

Jane hesitated, shook her head. "Sorry, Leslie; I don't think I could trust you on this. It should have been done a long, long time ago."

The Cadillac slipped noiselessly into the stream of traffic.

The caster's workshop was a dingy place, with plaster dust on the floor and the tools of his trade scattered around. He was a thin, middle-aged man in shirt sleeves with a long rubberized apron to protect his clothes.

He removed the last of the wrappings and looked at the

bas-relief while Leslie watched his face anxiously. At length he asked, "Who's the sculptor?"

"I am."

"You!" He stared at the slight girl incredulously. "This is brilliant work."

"Th-ank you."

He gave her a sharp look from behind bifocals. "You knew that, didn't you?"

"I—hoped—"

"Who taught you?"

"I had a year in New York and one in Paris. In New York I worked at an art school, in Paris at the studio of a good sculptor. I learned a lot from him, but then I found that I was beginning to see through his eyes, to copy his style, so I came home to work on my own, to find my own method. And then I couldn't seem to get the results that satisfied me and I see no purpose whatever in bad art, so I gave up. Then—I tried this."

He smiled. "You have every right to be proud of your work, young lady."

They discussed the casting and the materials. "All right," he said at last. "One week then, but it's going to be a rush." He held out his hand. "I'm happy to know you, Miss Blake. One of these days you'll be famous and I will boast that I knew you when."

As they walked down the dingy stairs from the second floor of the building, Doris squeezed Leslie's arm. "Famous! Jeepers, I'm so proud of you."

Leslie smiled. "Now where do we go?"

"Fittings," Doris said promptly.

For the next two hours, Doris stood and turned patiently, while a woman on her knees pinned and fitted, and two models, passing and repassing, took turns displaying evening dresses, afternoon dresses, suits.

"Oh, I forgot," Doris said to Leslie, who was busy making notes and sketching dresses, indicating colors. "I'll have to call Elizabeth Arden for a permanent. I want it two weeks before the wedding so I can have at least one shampoo before—oh, and gloves! Are there gloves on the list? Wait," she called to one of the models, "turn so I can see the back. Isn't that a love of a dress, Leslie? I've never worn black and white because I'm so dark but—"

A saleswoman came in, her arms filled with filmy slips, nightgowns, robes and housecoats. One by one, she held them up for Doris's inspection.

"That one," Doris said, "and that and—"

Leslie laughed. "Whoa! Hold it, Doris. Do you know how this thing is mounting up? I've been keeping a record. Eleven hundred dollars so far and there are still the basic things like—"

"It's all right," Doris said blithely. "Jane is footing the bills. Up to twenty-five hundred dollars. Plus the brides-maids' dresses."

"How—nice of her." Leslie tried to speak warmly, though she had been shoving the thought of Jane away frantically ever since she had left them, that odd purposeful look on her beautiful face.

Doris grinned impishly. "Well, after all, it's worth it to get rid of a sister who is ten years younger. I'm fond of Jane but I'm not fooled by her. She thinks of Jane first, last, all the time. You might remember that, too."

"What do you mean?"

The fitter had scrambled to her feet and carefully lifted the dress over Doris's head so as not to disarrange her hair. The models were temporarily out of the room. The saleswoman had gone in search of a white velvet housecoat. The two girls were alone.

"Jane is up to something," Doris said slowly. "I've never seen her the way she is now. She's gunning for you and she is loaded for bear."

"But why me?"

"I think you know why. Donald Shaw. When he first came here, he was out of his head about her. Then it—just dwindled away. Now she thinks he is in love with you. That has never happened to her before."

"But he—but she hates him."

"I don't think she knows how she feels about him. Especially now." Doris laughed. "She wants to be the heroine of the Clayton Festival, and hang on to Horace Fletcher, and keep Donald Shaw dangling. All at the same time. Like Bottom in *A Midsummer-Night's Dream,* she wants to play all the parts. That gal had better make up her mind."

"Where has she gone, Doris?" Leslie asked, hands gripping her sketchbook. "What can she possibly be planning to do?"

Doris gave her a quick look. "She is trying to lay a ghost. You're white as a sheet, Les. We'll take a break for lunch now."

The afternoon dragged on endlessly, though Leslie, as a rule, had a normal girl's delight in pretty clothes. Doris looked at handbags and hats and shoes. The list of purchases mounted and items were scratched off the list. The Babbling Brooke rippled merrily along.

"We'll live in the Logan house. In time, we'll probably make some changes but basically we'll leave it as it is. It's a darling Cape Cod and the old furniture is all authentic. Oh, Leslie, I wish you could be like this, simply bursting with happiness."

It was nearer six than five when they finally reached the Plaza to find Jane waiting impatiently. "Do you two know what time it is? I've been here over an hour."

Doris dropped into a chair beside her sister. "I've been so numb for the past three hours I don't even know what day it is."

"Then we had better have an early dinner in New York before we drive home," Jane said in resignation, "though there are never any interesting people in restaurants at this hour."

Over dinner Doris revived like a plant after watering. Leslie ate little, crumbling a roll in her fingers. She looked up to find Jane's big blue eyes on her face, a queer challenging expression in them.

Leslie straightened up, sipped a glass of water. "How did you spend the day?"

"I did some shopping of my own, visited an art gallery. And," Jane smiled, "I paid a visit to the Gypton Company."

"You—what!" Leslie set down the glass, the water splashing over the side.

Doris stared at her older sister. "Why did you do that?"

"Just a little idea of mine."

"What did you find out?"

Jane reached for the check. "All in good time," she said mockingly.

The ride home was a silent one. Doris was tired from long hours of standing, Jane was obstinately silent. After that one startling comment she had refused to amplify it in any way.

Leslie, alone on the back seat, sat with clenched hands. What had Jane found out about Donald Shaw? What was his association with the Gypton Company? All the evidence pointed in one direction, everything but the evidence of her own heart. She saw vividly in her memory the tall man whose dark hair was tinged with white, whose handsome face had lines of suffering and pain, but which warmed when he smiled, making his gray eyes glow, lighting a candle in her heart.

I love him, she told herself helplessly. There's just nothing to be done about it. I love him. In spite of everything, I believe in him.

The night was dark after they had left behind the lights of the city, then the less garish and more scattered lights of the suburbs. Now, off the parkway, they took a country road, the headlights tunneled under arching maples and elms, the road narrowed and curved as do most Connecticut roads. Jane's foot eased on the brake as they picked up two small lights, a raccoon standing on its hind legs, looking like a masked robber with its black-rimmed eyes.

"In the daytime," Doris said, the first to break the long silence, "I always forget that the woods are full of small animals. It's only at night I realize how—how alive they are."

"Raccoons won't hurt you," Jane said. "They wouldn't get anywhere attacking a human being. Their natural game is frogs and toads, little things like that."

"It isn't fear exactly. It's just that the woods seem to belong to all that animal life, not to us. That we are just intruders."

"Well, you don't have to go out in the woods at night," Jane reminded her. "It needn't bother you."

She slowed for a sharp curve. Across the double line a Volkswagen had stopped. There was a tire propped against it and a red flare blinked its caution. A man stood revealed by the flare. A woman moved, was in his arms, her hands behind his head, face lifted to his. As the Cadillac crept slowly past, the big headlights caught the man and woman, the man's black hair with its patches of white at the temples, the woman's red hair. The lights moved on around another curve.

"How stupid of her," Jane said coolly.

"Wasn't that Felice Allen?" Doris asked.

"And Mr. Donald Shaw." Jane pressed down on the gas pedal. The car leaped ahead until it reached the village, slowed for the Green and then turned onto the river road, halting before the Blake house.

"You look tired, Leslie," Jane said. "Sleep well." There was malice and a disturbing hint of triumph in her voice.

xvi

DONALD SHAW parked the Volkswagen behind Ye Olde Travelers' Rest and noticed in relief that there were no other cars. He experienced a momentary sense of rebellion. He was sick and tired of skulking around. But it couldn't be long now. The formula had been tested and retested. The end was nearly in sight.

Then what? He didn't know. The future remained a huge question mark. Wherever he turned there were obstacles, insurmountable barriers in his way. Play it by ear, he thought. Wait and see what happens next. "The best-laid plans of mice and men—"

By now he should be accustomed to being without roots, without a past or a future. Be grateful that he had a present. Be grateful to Dr. Forsyth that the man called Donald Shaw even existed.

"No one here," he said to Charlie Turgen. "We can talk freely. The food isn't good but I didn't think it would be wise for us to be seen together at the Fox and Rabbit."

"This will be fine," Charlie assured him.

When they had ordered, Donald asked, "How is your mother? Is her recuperation progressing satisfactorily?"

Charlie glowed. "Thanks to you letting me borrow the Volkswagen, I went to Edgeworth yesterday. It's a beautiful place. Lovely lawns and beautiful big lounging rooms with pleasant people to talk to. Mother has a delightful sunny bedroom. She's begun to gain weight and no wonder, for the food is out of this world. She is even getting a tan from sitting out of doors in the sun. She wrote to Mrs. Blake to try to express her gratitude. You knew that Mrs. Blake has been up there a couple of times to visit her?"

Donald shook his head. "I haven't seen the Blakes for several weeks."

"Mrs. Blake wouldn't even let Mother thank her. Said that was the very least she had a right to expect. And she talked about a job, librarian here in the village, that would pay twice as much as the cleaning. Mother would love it. Only, as she warned Mrs. Blake, she's a regular addict when it comes to reading. She's afraid she'd never get any work done if she were surrounded by books."

"That all sounds wonderful," Donald said heartily.

"Now—" Charlie reached in his pocket and pulled out a notebook.

"Eat that steak first," Donald told him. "All of it. There's plenty of time."

Charlie looked at the older man, friendly, relaxed, but carrying about him an intangible aura of command. He was really somebody. Aware that his hero worship would annoy his companion if he suspected it, Charlie devoted himself to his meal.

Over coffee and large wedges of apple pie and cheese, Donald said, "Now then."

Charlie flicked open his notebook. "First, Felice Allen. You know I made candid camera shots of everybody. I showed the one of her around the New York newspaper offices. A lot of people recognized her right away. She's who she says she is, all right. She really has a syndicated fashion column. She's been running it for about four years and each year she picks up more papers, so she is doing very well."

"I'd gathered that she was an efficient woman," Donald commented.

"Nothing known against her. Said to be a siren but no serious emotional interests. She came to New York from somewhere in the Midwest. Several people said she'd been married a couple of times but she's a widow. She prefers to be called 'Miss.' Allen was her husband's name."

"Allen," Donald said musingly.

"He's dead. Died several years ago. She lives alone in an expensive East Side apartment. Seen frequently at the smarter night spots and usually with different escorts. She seems to go chiefly for business reasons, to see what celebrities are wearing, get material for her column, all that."

"Business first," Donald agreed. "That's the way I summed her up, for all that Cleopatra, come-hither manner of hers."

"I called on a couple of the big-name couturiers, who spoke highly of her. She has *flair*, whatever that is, and her opinion on fashions carries a lot of weight in the trade. Some of the big designers even consult her before bringing out a new line." Charlie looked up. "Anything wrong?"

Donald shook his head, perplexed. "It's all straight-forward enough. There seems to be no doubt about her identity.

The trouble is that it doesn't throw any light on how she ties in with the situation here. A fashion expert who stays in a country village week after week. The searching of my room at the Fox and Rabbit. I have no proof but I am morally certain that she did it. Her attempts to find out from Wilcox and me what's going on in the Company. Her connection with Harrison. They are in something together—but what?"

Charlie consulted his notebook again. It was his job to collect the facts, not to draw conclusions from them.

"Second, Nors Swensen. He has lived in Claytonville all his life and worked for the Company since he was old enough to hold a job. Everyone has a good word for him. He was great pals with Douglas Clayton. Apparently from the time he could crawl he hung around Swensen, who kept an eye on him and, when he was old enough, took him camping and all that."

"Yes. Swensen told me much the same story himself."

"Lately, he's been sneaking off in his free time to the state police barracks. I didn't try to get anything out of Lieutenant Varelli," Charlie confessed. "I knew he wouldn't tell me anything."

Donald lighted a cigarette slowly. "Now I wonder," he began, "what that pig-headed Swede thinks he is doing. If he gums up the works, I'll take the skin off him."

"Want me to talk to him?" Charlie asked, with more courage than enthusiasm. Swensen would have made two of him.

"Leave him to me," Donald said grimly. "I might have known. The old fool!"

Charlie went back to his notes. "Third, Corliss Blake. Before he inherited the Clayton estate, he was an architect in Boston. Junior member of a firm that handled small jobs. Lately, with a go-getter in charge, a man who has 'contacts' in the local political machine, they're blossoming out and they've gathered in some real plums. Big contracts. Housing developments. All that. But, in his time, Blake didn't make much of an income. He eked out by teaching architecture in a smallish college. Married twice. The first wife died years ago and he nearly broke under it. Then he married Agatha Winslow. She was a great friend of his first wife. The Winslows had millions, both sides of the family terrifically wealthy, and she got the works. Nothing against her. And Blake went right on earning his own keep, you'll have to give him that."

Donald smiled at the boy's defiant tone. "You have every reason to be grateful to the Blakes. You don't need to defend yourself to me for liking the man. I like him myself."

Charlie looked relieved. "Fourth, James Mason." He paused dramatically.

Donald laughed outright, and his face became boyish and eager. "Give, man, give! You look like the cat that swallowed the canary. I can practically see the feathers on your mouth."

Charlie joined in the laughter. "This one is going to set you back on your heels. Jim Mason was formerly employed by—guess who?"

"The Gypton Company."

Charlie's face fell. "You knew it all the time," he accused him.

"I've just been putting two and two together."

"What are the other two?"

"Mason and Felice Allen. I'd bet anything that they are brother and sister. Same basic coloring. Same bone structure."

"Then Mason is the man who has been leaking information to Gypton?"

Donald hesitated. "Perhaps, though I'm damned if I can see how. He's no chemist."

"But he's responsible for that burglary?" Charlie's face hardened.

"I have a hunch that Mason worked on his own when he did that."

Charlie thought it out. "You mean he didn't intend to steal anything at all? It was a kind of trial run?"

"No," Donald said slowly. "I think it was meant as a warning."

"So he's the guy who stabbed my mother!"

"Quiet, Charlie."

"Quiet, nothing! Would you be quiet if he had clubbed and stabbed your mother?"

"If this is the kind of self-discipline you intend to offer the Federal Bureau of Investigation," Donald said in a tone of detachment, "you had better begin to plan on a different career. Frankly, they wouldn't give house room to a man who was bent on private vengeance."

A dull flush swept in a tide over Charlie's face. It was the first reproof he had received from the older man.

"Sorry," he muttered.

"Can you be relied on to keep your head? Not to take matters into your own hands? If you can't, you are of no further value to me."

"Sorry, Mr. Shaw. I really mean it and it won't happen again. But when I think of that guy—"

"Not think—*feel*. I understand how you feel. But now,

let's see a sample of how you can think." Donald grinned and terminated the moment's uneasiness between them.

"Okay, sir. Five, Oliver Harrison. Chemist with the Fromann Company in Cleveland. One of their top men. He'd have been head of the department in another few years but they work by the seniority system there. That's why he was willing to shift over to a smaller outfit. Less competition and a better chance of quick advancement, though he wouldn't make as much money in the long run."

"Unless he became president," Donald pointed out.

"Well, there's that, of course. But Blake is only in his fifties. It will be a long time—"

"Not if he is eased out," Donald told him.

"If he—" Charlie stared at him. "I think you have begun to see the pattern."

"Not altogether. I believe the original pattern was changed somewhere in the middle of the game. Could you run down any tie-in between Harrison and the Gypton people?"

"He never worked there, that's for sure. He went straight from college to Fromann. You think he is gunning for Blake's job?"

"Right now," Donald said mildly, "he is gunning for me. From the beginning he has attempted to undermine me. But today he went to Blake and tried his best to get me fired out of hand. He raised an awful stink. Their voices could be heard all over the Administration Building. At least three people have given me their versions of it. Apparently he has accused me of everything from A to Z, including general incompetence, dishonesty, staging the burglary, knocking out Nors, stabbing your mother, and trying to undercut Harrison himself."

"Is Blake going to do it?" Charlie asked tensely.

"No. He flatly refused."

"Good for him!"

"I wonder," Donald said thoughtfully. "Now I wonder."

*   *   *

The telephone was ringing when Donald Shaw let himself into his room at the Fox and Rabbit. As usual, he took a quick look around to see whether anything had been disturbed. Then he picked up the telephone.

A man's heavy voice spoke. "That you? This—"

"I know. Don't mention names, please."

"Someone else has horned in on the plan. Only way I can figure it out. Causing a lot of heart-burning here at Gypton."

"You're sure?"

"No, I can't be sure. I'm playing it blind. But that's the way it looks. If there are two groups at work, it is going to be an unholy mess."

"I can imagine."

"Keep your eyes open," the heavy voice warned.

"I hardly dare close them to go to sleep." Donald laughed.

"Oh, by the way, did you know we've had some inquiries here about you?"

"About me?"

"One Donald Shaw. Was he ever employed here? What is known about his background, his record, and so forth, and so forth. Very determined woman. Refused to be put off."

"Woman!" Donald ejaculated. "Did you see her?"

"In person. My name's on the bulletin board downstairs and she asked for me."

"Hmm. Makes it awkward, doesn't it?"

"Time is running out on you, my boy."

"Don't I know it! How much did you tell that alluring redhead?"

"Redhead?"

"Didn't she have red hair? Name of Felice Allen?"

"No. She was a blonde. And a beauty. Name of Williams. Mrs. John Williams." After a long pause, the heavy voice said sardonically, "I gather that I have shaken you."

"You've knocked me for a loop," Donald admitted. "You've got my head spinning."

"Brace yourself. The worst is yet to come. I've been asked to go up to Claytonville and expose you publicly."

"And what," Donald asked, "did you say to that?"

"Oh," the heavy voice said cheerfully, "I can never refuse anything to a beautiful woman. I agreed, of course." He chuckled. "Good night!"

Donald set down the telephone. Before he could move away, it rang again.

"Donald?" drawled a husky voice.

"Felice," he exclaimed with exaggerated pleasure. "How nice of you." He added mendaciously, "I was just about to call you."

"Well, well, so I've broken you down at last! Dinner tonight?"

"Eight o'clock?" he suggested.

"Fine. I'll see you in the lobby."

He shaved and changed quickly, determined that this time he would be the one to ask the questions and wondering, a trifle dismally, just how he was going to dispose of another dinner on top of the hearty one he had finished a scant half-hour ago.

Felice, in a thin black dress, sleeveless and low cut, her red hair hatless and done in an extreme style, make-up smooth and flawless, exuding a faint but expensive perfume, was evidently prepared to move in for the kill.

The narrow green eyes surveyed him with approval. "What the well-dressed man should wear. You're a very distinguished escort."

"Madam, your servant," he said with an exaggerated, courtly bow.

"You'd have been stunning in Renaissance clothing. It would have suited your type."

How much of this stuff did she expect him to swallow? Evidently, in her experience, there was no limit to a man's vanity.

"You should see me in my suit of armor," he said lightly. He helped her into the Volkswagen, aware of the battery of eyes from the rocking chair brigade.

"We're giving them quite a thrill," Felice said with a laugh.

"Poor things, if second-hand thrills are all they have, they're welcome. Where would you like to go?"

She named the most expensive restaurant within practicable driving distance and he mentally checked his billfold to be sure he had money enough to cover the charges.

"Fine! That will give me time for a pleasant drive with you."

They chatted aimlessly for a while. But Felice Allen wasn't a woman to let an opportunity go to waste.

"Whatever happened about that burglary?" she asked. "It just seems—to an outsider, at least—as though the whole investigation had petered out."

"That's about the way it is," he said.

"What do you think was behind it?"

He shrugged. "No idea."

"I understand Mr. Corliss Blake practically admitted that it was an inside job."

"So he did," Donald agreed amiably.

"Oh, Donald, I could shake you! You are so exasperating."

In the darkness he grinned to himself. "I'm not being mysterious. I just don't know anything about it. The state police haven't taken me into their confidence."

"Well, I think it's a shame, when I consider the way you took over at the time. Right on the spot. And stood guard all night. They owe you some consideration."

"Things really get around, don't they?"

For a moment she showed a trace of discomposure. "Oh, you know how villages are. Little things get all out of proportion."

"I still can't figure you in a village, Felice. You are Park Avenue and café society if I ever saw it. What on earth do you find to interest you here, week after week?"

Apparently she was accustomed to men who were delighted to talk about themselves, who let her control the direction of the conversation. She hesitated for a moment, as though feeling her way. Then she said, with the least convincing attempt at shyness he had ever encountered, "Don't you know, darling?"

To his relief, they had reached the restaurant and a boy ran out to park the car for them. Seeing the little Volkswagen among the Cadillacs, Lincolns and Jaguars, Donald grinned.

"I was afraid for a moment that boy would be too superior to park it."

During dinner he kept the conversation flowing lightly but agreeably, maintaining firm control over it and steering it as he chose. Exasperated as she was by his competent technique, Felice found herself entertained and surprised into frequent laughter. After all, he was a singularly handsome man, he had an amusing wit, and she was aware that they attracted a good deal of attention and admiration.

None the less, she was aware, too, of the man's inner amusement at her frustration, and though it infuriated her she found herself more genuinely interested in him than she had been before.

It wasn't until they were back in the little car and he pulled over to make way for a driver in a hurry, his attention on the passing car, that she took advantage of his momentary distraction to ask, "And how's the Great Affair coming along?"

"What great affair?"

"You and the Blake girl."

"There's no affair. I haven't even seen her for some time. Why should you suppose—" For the first time she had got under his skin and there was an edge on his voice.

"Sorry, Donald. I'm really sorry. I was just baiting you, trying to get even."

"I don't know what you are driving at."

"Why do you make me do it all?" There was a throb in her husky voice. "You must know how I feel about you. You're the most attractive man I ever met. And yet you act—you pretend—"

"Felice! Stop ribbing me."

"I'm not. Oh, about the Blake girl—yes. I knew you'd lost out there and I suppose I was just trying to get my own back. The news is all over town. She is going to marry Oliver Harrison. The girl *and* the business. He's really got his future all laid out, hasn't he?" There was anger in her tone.

"Has he?"

"Don't pretend you weren't after her, too! The Clayton money and the Winslow fortune. Nice pickings. Very nice. But Oliver Harrison will get what he wants. He always has."

"Do you know him as well as that?" Donald sounded extremely surprised. "I had no idea that you were such old acquaintances."

Felice took her time lighting a cigarette. She drew on it, watching the tip glow red in the darkness. One hand came up to stroke his cheek softly.

"Watch your step, Donald, darling. The inn is a rumor factory. I heard today that the Harrison man is after your scalp. He's trying to get you fired."

"I won't worry about that until I know how Corliss Blake feels about it."

"Blake will do as he is told," Felice said flatly. "You can be sure of that."

The car swerved across the road and Donald fought the wheel. It swerved again. "A flat!" he said in disgust.

"But it's a brand-new car," Felice protested.

In spite of his annoyance, Donald had to laugh outright. "Lady, a nail doesn't know that the tire is new."

He pulled as far off the narrow road as he could, set up flares, and jacked up the side of the little car. He took off the tire, propped it against the body and got out the spare.

Then Felice was beside him. Suddenly she was in his arms. The headlights of a big car illuminated them as though they stood in a spotlight. Instead of moving away, her arms went around him, her hands on the back of his head drew him close to her. Her lips touched his.

The big car moved slowly past on the narrow curve, then it was gone. Felice dropped her hands and stepped back. She laughed softly.

"Crisis! Scandal! This little indiscretion is going to be all over the village by morning. Did you see who they were?"

Donald stooped to put on the tire. He tightened bolts. "No, I didn't see them."

"Mrs. Williams was driving. And in the back seat—all eyes—was your boss's daughter."

"And just what," Donald asked evenly, "was the purpose of that performance, Felice?"

She laughed. "Don't you know why?"

"Let's stop playing games, shall we? You aren't interested in me. Just what are you trying to do?"

"If you can't guess, I'm not going to help you out."

"You'd be surprised to know how much I've guessed," he said without expression. He took the jack apart, held the car door for her.

She got in without a word, but when he put the key in the switch her hand covered his, checked him. "Donald, don't be so difficult. Can't you be nice to me?" There was laughter in her tone now. "After all, there's no one to see. The rocking chair brigade is preparing for bed. Can't you just imagine the chin straps, the wrinkle eradicators, the cold cream, the hair nets? We are alone, darling."

"Not really alone, are we?"

"What do you mean?" Instinctively, she peered out of the car, her voice startled.

"I was thinking of your partners," he said pleasantly. "You're being rather stupid, Felice. There is always trouble brewing when thieves fall out."

LESLIE called a greeting to her father and Agatha, who were in the drawing room.

"I'm too tired to breathe," she exclaimed. "I think we visited every shop, big and small, in New York City. Visited! We combed them, floor by floor, aisle by aisle. I'm off to bed."

"How about your sculpture?" Agatha asked, coming eagerly out into the hallway as Leslie began to climb the stairs. She pulled herself up wearily as though they were as high as Jack's beanstalk. "I've wondered all day what the caster had to say."

"He liked it. He really liked it."

"How could he help it!" Agatha exclaimed.

Leslie turned to blow her a kiss. "You're a honey," she said gratefully. "I was just dying to have someone ask about it so I could boast a little. Now my ego is satisfied. Good night." She looked down the stairs. "Good night, Mother."

She went up quickly, the lights blurring for her as they must be blurring in Agatha's eyes, which had filled with tears.

Leslie turned on taps in her bathroom and took a long leisurely tub that ironed out the fatigue in her body but not the pain in her heart. The events of the day had been canceled out by the moment when, in the light of a red flare, she had seen Felice Allen in Donald Shaw's arms.

She slid on a terry cloth robe and went to look out her bedroom window. At length, she tossed off the robe, dressed in a dark skirt and shirt and tennis shoes, and stole down the stairs. Her father and Agatha were still talking in the drawing room. They would hear the front door open. In her father's study she softly opened the French doors and stepped out on the lawn. She walked quietly down toward the river, sank on the grass and lay flat, looking up at the sky.

There was no moon but the stars shone the more brightly.

The big dipper was brilliant tonight. Her eyes moved from one contellation to another. The immensity which the universe represented was beyond comprehension. She lived on a small planet circling the sun, in one of countless galaxies. As an individual, in space and time, she was infinitely small. She told herself all this, slowly and carefully. She didn't matter against the infinity of space and time.

But she did matter. Every human being mattered. That was true, too. The flight of a bird took seconds, the life of a rose was a matter of a few days. But they mattered.

Leslie sat up. She couldn't escape from her dilemma by a plunge into space. Short as her life was, insignificant perhaps, it was all she had. But she must make the best accounting for it that she could. She couldn't pretend her pain did not exist. She had to come to terms with it.

She clasped her hands around her knees, looking down at the dark mass of the barge on the river. This was where Douglas Clayton had played as a small boy, where he had dreamed dreams and played pirate like Jack Williams, conquered imaginary foes and planned the life which he had, in the end, deliberately sacrificed for others.

It was curious, she thought, that what people remembered was Douglas Clayton the hero, not Douglas Clayton the gay, lighthearted boy he must have been. She stared at the barge and blinked. She wiped her eyes but the light was still there, flickering. A fairy light. Unreal. The skin on her arms turned to gooseflesh. She heard her own voice saying, "If Douglas Clayton haunts any place, it is the barge."

Her heart was beating irrationally. She was tempted to race for the house, shut out that light. The light that wasn't there, that couldn't be there. Instead, she took a long breath and went steadily down the lawn to the river's edge.

The light flashed again. A flashlight. Ghosts don't carry flashlights. She was beginning to shake but she made herself go on, groped for the rope that moored the barge, scrambled up.

"Who's there?" she asked in a low voice that would not carry to the house.

There was a gasp. The torch moved, caught her in a noose of light. Then there was darkness.

"Who's there?" she repeated, a betraying quaver in her tone.

"Leslie, I'm sorry. It's Donald. I didn't meant to frighten you." A hand touched her hair, her arm.

"Donald!" Her voice was still low. "What on earth are you doing here?"

"I couldn't sleep. I came for a walk down here by the

river. Then I remembered what you had said about the barge. I was just exploring. Do you mind?"

"Of course not. Well—good night."

"Don't go yet." He did not touch her again but his voice held her, charmed her. She could not move. Then his voice changed, lost its warmth. "I understand that congratulations are in order."

"Why?"

"On your approaching marriage to Harrison."

"But I'm not going to marry Oliver Harrison," she exclaimed in indignation. "Where did you hear that?"

"From Felice Allen. She told me that it is common knowledge to everyone in the village."

"Except to me." She turned away.

"Hold on! Please, Leslie. Don't go. Not just yet. We've never really talked. I meant to wait—if the time ever came—but I can't let you go like this, not with such absurd misunderstandings between us."

His hand groped for hers, closed on it, and he guided her to a bench. "He won't mind our being here," he told her softly.

"Who won't?"

"Douglas Clayton. If this was really his sanctuary and he still haunts it, I think he would welcome us." He spoke as though addressing the ghost that haunted the barge: "Rest, rest, perturbed spirit."

In the dark of the night there were quiet murmurs. Water lapped gently against the barge. Leaves moved sibilantly, as though whispering to each other. In the sky the stars wheeled on their timeless journey. And still the man beside her did not speak. Leslie waited, wondering if he could hear her quickened breathing, the thud of her heart that seemed like the pounding of surf, thunderous in the night.

"Two misunderstandings," he began suddenly.

"You don't owe me any explanations, Donald," she said.

"Yes, I do. I believe you know that. You know why. I love you, Leslie. I believe you know that, too. That is why there must be no more misunderstandings between us. There is no disloyalty or discourtesy on my part in clearing things up. First, there was Jane Williams's dramatic reaction when she found me kissing you. There was—no occasion for it. There is nothing between Jane Williams and me, Leslie. Nothing at all."

"But there was," she said.

"Yes, there was." His voice sounded tired. "There was all the magic of moonlight. But it's gone now. Even if there hadn't been you, there were the little things. Her dismay when she knew her son would be playing around again in a few days. Her disregard for everyone but herself. Her colossal and self-centered vanity. Her—cruelty."

Leslie stirred in the darkness, remembering how Jane had run from him, with revulsion in her face, when she saw the scars on his scalp.

"The other thing," he said quietly, "that silly incident to-night—Felice Allen staged the whole business. She was playing a game of her own. I'm not sure what it is, though I'd back my guesses and they have nothing to do with me. The point I'm trying to make is that she is of no importance. She—remember the talk we had that night when I kissed you? Your father had told you that your mother was like the sun shining on the Garden of Eden."

She made no reply. His hand tightened on hers.

"Felice Allen is—just lamplight. But I want sunlight. I've been afraid of the sun for a long time but now I need it. The sunlight that is you, Leslie."

She tried to speak but she could not utter a sound.

His arms gathered her close, his lips brushed her hair. "I want your love. Some day, I hope, I trust, I can ask you for it. But now I need your trust even more, perhaps, than your love."

He waited a long time for her to speak. Then it was he who broke the silence.

"I'm sorry; I asked too much of you. I didn't have the right. Forgive me if you can."

She turned to him then. His fingers touched her cheek.

"Tears! You're crying! What have I done? I didn't mean to distress you, to cause you the slightest bit of unhappiness."

"It's—" She caught her breath and then said bravely, "It's not unhappiness. You remember those words of Wordsworth: 'Surprised by joy.' "

"Leslie," he said huskily. He lifted her chin, found her mouth, kissed her. "Leslie, what have I done to deserve this?"

"People don't deserve love," she said, out of that new and sweet knowledge of hers. "They just accept it when it comes. They welcome it—if it is right for them."

"Am I—right for you?"

She drew back from his ardent kiss with a breathless laugh. "I think you must be. Don't you?"

"And you don't even know anything about me," he said in a shaken voice.

"Lots of things," she said confidently. "All the important things."

"Such as?" She could hear the smile in his voice.

"That you have suffered without growing hard; that you can be magnanimous, even to people who are unfair to you; that you have a gift for laughter to help keep you on an even keel; that you're a man of integrity."

"You know all that?" he whispered, his cheek brushing hers. His arms tightened abruptly and then, just as abruptly, he released her. He helped her to her feet.

"I'm coming back soon to ask you to marry me. But, meanwhile, you're going to need all your faith in me. I hope it's strong enough."

"It's strong enough," she said confidently.

"It will need to be," he warned her. "I'll see you as soon as I can. It won't be long."

"But why can't you—"

"That's what I meant by trust, my beloved. No questions. Just blind faith."

"All right. I'll be waiting."

She ran up the lawn in the dark, her heart singing. This is happiness, she told herself. The poets were always right. "Surprised by joy."

She let herself quietly into the house, not even aware that the French doors stood wide open on the night. She turned once to look back. There was a flash of light on the barge that was quickly extinguished.

*　　*　　*

"I thought you had gone to bed!"

Leslie started as she heard her father's voice. He had been sitting in the dark.

"I couldn't sleep," she told him, "and it's much cooler down by the river."

"I couldn't sleep either," he said. "I've almost forgotten what it's like to have a sound night's sleep."

She curled up at his feet. "You can't keep this up, Dad, or you'll have a breakdown."

"It's nearly over," Corliss Blake said. "In one more week we should be ready to go into production. If we can hold the Gypton Company off that long. Once we've announced the new formula and entered the market they won't be able to stop us. And then—" He sighed. "Then I'll feel that I have done my job and I'll be able to retire. Harrison can take over if he likes."

"You don't really like Oliver, do you, Dad?"

"He has made my position intolerable ever since that abortive burglary. I feel sure that he has started rumors about my complicity in the affair."

"Dad!"

"And he has tried, in every way he can think of, to drive me out of the Company."

"Then why should you retire and let him have his own way?" Leslie protested hotly.

"Whatever he is as a man," her father told her, "and personally I hate his guts, he is a fine chemist. He is better fitted for the job of leadership than I am. I've always felt like a square peg in a round hole at the Company. That's why I have let Harrison have his head as much as I have. I wanted to test him, to see what he was made of, how he would react to situations, how he could handle a big job."

He paused to consider. "I don't like the way he abuses his authority, but he's an ambitious man. His heart is set on being president of the Clayton Textile Company. It's quite possible, with a man of his type, that once he has acquired the power he seeks so desperately, he'll be easier to deal with. It often works that way. As president he'd do everything he could to insure its success."

"But to give such a splendid opportunity to a man who tries to undermine you," Leslie said furiously. "It just isn't fair!"

"He has found that there are limits," her father said. "Over and over, he has tried his best to get Shaw fired but I have stood pat. Of course, when Harrison takes command, as I assume he is bound to do eventually, Shaw will be out in a flash. But that will no longer be my concern."

"Dad, about that burglary—"

"I don't know, Puss. I simply don't know. I have an unpleasant suspicion—"

"Please tell me."

"That the state police know more about it than they have been willing to tell me."

"You mean they don't trust you?"

"I don't know what they think," he confessed. "All I am sure of is that Harrison is in the clear on that business. He was in this house, under my own eyes, when the incident took place. Everyone has told me the same story, that he was genuinely shocked and surprised." He added slowly, "And Donald Shaw, on the other hand, was at the laboratory where he had no reason to be. There is no getting away from the fact." His hand pressed her shoulder.

"Nors Swensen knows something he isn't telling," Leslie said.

"He has told the police."

"You're sure?"

"He hustled away with them the night of the burglary and

he has avoided me as much as possible ever since. He is trying to escape having a showdown."

"And—Donald?"

"The state police have talked with him, of course. After Harrison's public statement, which was practically an accusation, he volunteered to answer their questions. I don't know, Leslie. I just don't know. Personally, I like the man. As you know, I gambled on him in the beginning. And I do not intend to condemn him without proof. It's not that I am defending my own judgment; I believe in giving any man a fair chance to clear himself."

He sat straighter in his chair and dismissed the subject. "You ought to get some rest. This is going to be a frenzied week. Next Sunday we'll hold the Clayton Festival and on Monday the public announcement will be made about the formula. Try not to worry, Leslie. Things have a way of working out. Perhaps not the way we hope, but well enough. I'm sorry."

"Sorry?"

"You're too young to have to learn the bitter lesson that living is a lonely business."

Because she was happy in her love, Leslie was eager to reach out and share from her own wealth. Perhaps only happy people are capable of full generosity. The unhappy are engrossed in themselves, and happiness comes only with self-forgetfulness.

"Dad," she said impulsively, "life doesn't have to be lonely. There is something I've wanted to tell you for a long time, but I didn't know how. About Aunt Agatha. About—Mother."

The words tumbled out as she told him of that revealing talk with her stepmother. He did not interrupt.

When she came to a stop, he got up. "I'm glad you told me, dear. So blind! How could I have been so blind? She never asked anything of me. I thought she was contented. I—Good night, Puss. Get some sleep. You've a wild week ahead."

She went up to her room. Some time later, she heard her father's steps on the stairs. He mounted slowly but purposefully. He passed his own room. At Agatha's door ne paused. Then he knocked.

xviii

IN some way, the following week seemed to slip by like greased lightning. Everyone in the laboratory at the Clayton Textile Company was working at top speed with a mounting frenzy of excitement as the goal loomed in sight. At night, the chemists were haggard and exhausted, but the exhilaration of success kept them buoyed up.

Every night a prowl car patrolled the Company grounds, coming at irregular and unscheduled hours. Nors Swensen plodded on his usual rounds. He had completely recovered from his accident but he had acquired a new wariness, a sharper lookout. Charlie Turgen had volunteered to go on night duty with him.

Everyone was aware of a tightening of nerves. Just one week more, just four more days, just three. Finally, only one day remained.

The men in the laboratory worked like demons. For once, they did not object to Harrison's relentless drive. They were eager to give him all he asked for, all they had in them. Their common objective forged the kind of bond that one usually finds only in a small corps of men sweating it out under gunfire in wartime. The "all for one and one for all" of the Three Musketeers.

Donald Shaw ended every day in a fog of fatigue, more acutely aware than all but one other person of the extent of the possible explosion ahead. He was too tired to protest when Charlie Turgen insisted on accompanying him back to the Fox and Rabbit every night before he went on guard duty, though he thought the precaution absurd. It was unlikely that he was in any danger, but he let Charlie have his own way and, in response to Charlie's pleas, he remained in his room in the evenings, though the nights were hot and sultry.

Sitting in the dark by his open window, night after night, he was able to cast off his exhaustion only when he let himself think of Leslie. "Surprised by joy." Leslie, who had given him the unhoped-for treasure of her love and a steady undeviating faith. Whatever the revelations of the future, she would be steadfast. He wondered, humbly, what he had done to merit her faith and her love.

Sometimes, on the brink of sleep, he dared to imagine what their lives might be together in the future: Leslie to come home to at night, with her warmth and her sweetness and the occasional erratic emotional upheavals that made her so unpredictable. "Her infinite variety," he thought. Certainly it would never cease to enchant him.

He remembered her long patient nursing of Jack Williams. What a mother she would be! Even if he lived to be a very old man, he would not have time to show her all the love and tenderness he felt for her.

Now and then, he was aroused from his preoccupation with Leslie and with the final steps in perfecting the formula to an awareness of the unusual activities going on in the village for the Clayton Festival, and particularly in the Green below his window. Bunting was being tacked up. Shop windows were being decorated with flags and pictures of Douglas Clayton. All day, women poured in and out of the Town Hall, where long tables were being set up and preparations were being made for the supper that was to follow the speeches and to precede the showing of the documentary of the Tower Heights offensive.

Up to now, the preparations had stirred in him only an amused wonder, but as he became conscious of their extent, of the seriousness with which they were being made, he was alarmed. Something ought to be done to stop the whole thing, he thought.

A grandstand was being constructed on the Green, attended by much hammering and shouting, and with half the small boys of the village getting under the feet of the workmen. A site had been prepared for the bas-relief, which was to be placed on the Green in honor of Douglas Clayton.

Only one day left, Donald thought, sprawled in an easy chair with his legs swung over the arm. After that, he would sleep for a week. If he hadn't forgotten how.

The shrill ringing of the telephone startled him in the quiet room and he stretched out an arm to silence it.

"Shaw speaking."

"This is Charlie Turgen." The boy's voice was charged with excitement. "Come fast."

"They've tried it again?" Donald asked sharply.

"No, there's a fire. I'm putting in a call for the Volunteer Fire Department. Hurry!"

"On my way." Donald slammed down the telephone, caught

up his jacket, groped for billfold and car keys and ran. By the time the Volkswagen had reached the covered bridge he heard behind him the hoarse toots that summoned the volunteer firemen. He could picture clearly what was happening in the quiet village behind him. Young men were leaving the movies or their television sets or their night jobs, running to climb on the fire engine or piling into their own cars, everything from Lincolns to trucks, dinner clothes to over-alls, lights blinking as they raced to face the common enemy of a village set in the woods, the eternal menace of fire.

As the Volkswagen emerged from the bridge, and it had never seemed so long to him before, though it was one of the longest covered bridges in New England, Donald looked toward the Company buildings, half expecting to see them ablaze.

Everything was dark and still. Had he been called out on a hoax? Then he looked toward the river. Something like a huge birthday cake with candles was on the river, moving slowly toward him.

For a moment Donald stared in bewilderment. Then he understood. It was the barge, which had broken loose from its moorings, and was drifting down the river toward the covered bridge, ablaze with light. Someone had set fire to it.

In a flash, the whole pattern became clear to him. He knew now why Jim Mason had patrolled the river in his canoe, studying the barge and its position in relation to the Company. The fire was designed to provide a distraction while the real, the final attempt was made to steal the formula.

At the parking lot Donald got out of the Volkswagen and began to run. He could see moving lights now, flashlights used by men who were racing toward the river and the blazing barge, running away from the laboratory. He turned straight toward the building, tore around to the back. A window had been smashed open. He turned on lights, racing from room to room. In the room where the data on the formula had been locked up, a cabinet had been broken open, the drawers were empty.

Too late, he thought. Too late. But where is Charlie? Where is Nors? How did they let themselves be taken off guard like this?

Whoever had stolen the formula had got away with it. That was Donald's sick conviction. The laboratory was empty. He threw open the front door, heard a car motor race, heard a car move off. All this had happened before, he thought.

There were running feet. Someone cannonaded into Don-

ald, veered away from him and was off like a deer. There
was something dark on the ground, a long bundle. This had
happened before, too. Donald stumbled, nearly fell over it.
He dropped to his knees, bent over the prostrate figure,
raised the shoulders, pushed back a hat from a face streaked
with blood.

"Nors!" he cried. "Nors!"

Feet pounded toward him and a flashlight pinned Donald
against the darkness as he bent over the unconscious man.

"That you, Shaw?"

Donald recognized the voice. "You're right on the spot,
thank God! Lieutenant Varelli, they've got away with it and
Nors—"

The lieutenant knelt beside him, turned the man over
gently. "That's not Swensen. That's the head chemist, Mr.
Harrison." His fingers groped over the man's head, came away
sticky with blood.

Oliver opened his eyes, blinked at the light, stared at the
two men bending over him.

"I—saved the formula," he said with an effort. "It's in
my pocket—no, the other side." He waited while Varelli retrieved the papers. Then Harrison looked at Donald. His
voice was stronger, clearer. "Arrest this man. He's the one
who attacked me."

Varelli put a whistle to his lips. Two more troopers came
running. "Get him to the hospital," he said. "He may have
concussion or even a skull fracture."

"We'll have to go the long way round," one of the troopers
said. "The barge had wedged against the center support of
the covered bridge and the thing is on fire. Only way back
is Route 13 behind the Company."

Varelli grinned broadly. "Well, well," he said. "Someone
sure miscalculated this time. Have roadblocks set up on
Route 13. This is going to catch someone off balance."

One of the troopers ran back to the radio car to carry
out his orders. Varelli told the other one to guard Harrison
until they could move him.

"Someone," he explained, "doesn't like this guy very much
and may possibly come back for another try."

The lieutenant turned for a long look at Donald, who was
standing beside him. "Waiting for something?" he asked
gravely, though his eyes were dancing.

"I thought, after Harrison's accusation, you'd put me under
arrest."

"Did you hit him?"

"No, of course not. I found him like that, but—"

"Then suppose you run along and help the boys with that

barge. The firemen can't reach it with their equipment from that side. What we need is a fireboat. The whole bridge is going to go. Too bad. I like to see these old landmarks."

Donald's reactions were slowed by fatigue and the shock of Harrison's statement. "Then you aren't going to arrest me?"

The lieutenant shook his head.

"Why not?"

"Fingerprints, Mr. Shaw," the lieutenant said gently. "Very interesting things, fingerprints. And a report from the War Department."

Harrison had lapsed into unconsciousness by the time the troopers had lifted him into their patrol car. Nors Swensen came running up.

"Who got hurt?"

"Harrison," Donald told him.

"Good," Swensen declared heartily. "It's serious, I devoutly hope."

"Where were you when the laboratory window was smashed."

"Out here conferring with Varelli."

"You mean he's been on duty here all evening?"

"Every night this week. We've been expecting trouble. Only that burning barge threw us off at first." Nors chuckled. "It was meant to provide a distraction. Instead, it is burning the bridge and the only escape route straight back to the village, unless they swim for it. Now they've got to take Route 13 and cross the river eight miles up the road. Roadblocks are probably up already."

"Had it all worked out, didn't you?" Donald said, open suspicion in his voice.

Nors grinned. "I told you I'm a good guard."

Donald found himself grinning reluctantly at the man's sheer impudence. "Smart guy, aren't you? But where is Charlie Turgen?"

"I don't know. He ran to call you and the volunteer firemen. Then he went back to the river. He yelled something. Sounded like he said there was someone on the barge. He was going to try to swim for it."

"Someone on the barge. Good God!" Donald looked at the blazing mass that rocked against the center support of the bridge. Sparks were shooting up from the top of the bridge now. On the far side, firemen were shouting, running, trying to direct a stream of water onto the bridge, since they could not reach the barge.

In a moment a puff of wind tore the smoke aside like a flimsy veil. There were two figures on the barge at the end farthest from the blaze, a slim figure with rounded lines, a very small angular one. A girl and a small child.

Donald bent to tear off his shoes, to strip down to shorts. Then he raced down to the river and plunged in.

". . . after Scotland, Paris," Doris said dreamily. "Then Rome and Venice and the Riviera and the Greek islands. Home by Christmas."

"Just about time enough for you to finish tacking that bunting," Leslie said dryly.

Doris laughed. "Well, if you were being married in three weeks—"

"You get to work or I'll step in and forbid the banns or whatever they do. Why, even Jane has done more work than you have today. She's supervised the decorating of the tables, and got supplies of dishes and silverware and even arranged the seating. And that, let me tell you, is no small job. What with everyone in the village demanding to be given precedence and a choice seat. Now I know what it must be like for the State Department protocol people to seat a White House dinner."

"Hey," Paul protested from the entrance to the Town Hall, "stop working my bride to death." He took the hammer and nails from Doris and climbed the ladder to tack up the bunting. "If you want my considered opinion, for which you have failed to ask me, this Clayton Festival is wearing me to the bone."

Leslie, fanning herself with a paper plate, laughed at the young man, who was in the pink of condition.

"And what civic duty have you been performing?"

"I've been drilling the high school fife and drum corps. The fife is fast becoming my least favorite instrument. Have you heard about the Great Crisis?"

"What now?" Leslie asked in resignation.

"Miss Eustace wants to make the oration at the Festival because she's an authority on the Clayton family."

"Oh, no," Leslie and Doris wailed in unison.

"Oh, yes," Paul assured them. "There was a horrible and blood-curdling moment when I thought she'd got away with

it. I could just picture the villagers fainting in droves from
sheer boredom as she launched well into her stride in the
fourth hour of her oration."

"What's to be done?" Leslie exclaimed in despair. "This
is disaster."

"Paul," Doris said in excitement, "I know what. You'll
have to kidnap her. Just for the evening, of course."

"Hark to the wench! I always thought she'd have me em-
barked on a life of crime before I knew it. Anyhow," he added
dramatically, "the day is saved."

"How?"

"Mrs. Blake." Paul laughed. "You know, Les, that stepmother of yours is quite a gal. She has my vote. Everyone
was looking pale and stricken and she spoke up firmly and
said it would be a great pity to waste that wonderful material, and that, anyhow, no mere speech could do it justice.
The audience would be too limited. She knew everyone
would agree with her in thinking that Miss Eustace should
put the whole thing in writing, have it printed, and then
it would attract the wide distribution it deserved and be of
lasting historical value."

"Your stepmother deserves a medal," Doris declared fervently. "Oh, dear, here comes Mrs. Hastings with some more
of those ghastly prizes. I do wish she could remember what
committee she is serving on. Now she seems to think the
Festival is to be an athletic contest. What are we going to
do with her?"

"She can give prizes for the best fife and drum corps,"
Paul said promptly. "That won't strain her because there is
only one of them, anyhow. Thank the lord! I'll be a hero
and sidetrack her." He climbed down from the ladder and
went to meet the woman who had her arms filled with
oddly wrapped packages.

"But who really will make the speeches?" Doris asked.

"The Governor is coming over to make the oration. His
son was in Douglas Clayton's company. And Nors Swensen
is going to talk informally, reminiscing about him as a boy."

"And your sculpture?"

"It will be delivered and set up in the morning. Jane, of
course, is going to unveil it," Leslie said rather dryly.

"Her big moment," Doris commented. "She is out riding
with Horace Fletcher right now. Trying to mend her fences."

"Why? Anything wrong between them? I thought he adored
her. Treated her as though she were made of Venetian glass."

Doris grinned. "So he did. But he's a child specialist. Remember? And he has eyes in his head. He has begun to see

that Jane doesn't really care a fig for Jack. When you are too busy to play with him, or Paul and I go off somewhere, he just wanders around by himself. I don't believe the doctor likes it much. Poor little mite! Jack needs other children to play with but Jane doesn't want them around. They make too much noise. So Captain Blood has to depend on imaginary companions."

*   *   *

When Leslie got home, she found a note on the hall table: "Leslie dear, your father and I are dining alone at Litchfield tonight to get away from all the problems. I've let the maids off for the day and evening because they have volunteered to help serve at the Festival supper. There are chicken salad, cucumber sandwiches and iced tea in the refrigerator. Love." The note was signed "Mother."

Leslie smiled as she read it. Perhaps Agatha Blake would never take the place of her predecessor but she had made a real place of her own. She had acquired a new radiance and a new softness. And Corliss Blake had changed, too. He was happier, more confident and expansive than Leslie ever remembered him to be. All of a sudden he and Agatha had discoverd a host of mutual interests, their conversation had a new eagerness, they caught each other's eyes to share thoughts and impressions.

When she had eaten her cold supper, Leslie went out on the lawn. Usually there was a cool breeze in the evenings by the river, but tonight not a leaf stirred. The air was still hot and sultry. It had an oppressive, foreboding quality.

She curled up on the lawn. Even that felt dry and warm. She looked down at the barge, remembering the night, a week before, when she had discovered Donald Shaw there and found love with all its grandeur, all its simplicity. Some day, he was coming back for her. Some day. Any day. Perhaps tomorrow.

A light flickered on the barge. She scrambled to her feet. He was there now! She began to run. Then there seemed to be a dozen lights burning at once. Flames were shooting up from the river. And above the roar of the flames came the high desperate scream of a panic-stricken child.

Jack Williams was trapped on the blazing barge. She was at the water's edge, but the barge had broken free from its mooring, there was a widening expanse of water. She slipped out of her shoes, unzipped her dress, stepped out of it, and plunged into the river.

Again she heard that shrill, terrified scream.

"Captain Blood!" she called, lifting her head out of the water. "Captain Blood!"

"L-Leslie?"

"I'm coming to report, Captain. The crew is on duty. You stand guard. Don't move."

"Aye, aye, sir," said the small, frightened voice.

A few more strokes and her fingers touched the side of the barge, clawed at it. She got a toehold, heaved herself up, gathered into her arms the shivering small boy, giving him the comfort he so badly needed.

He clung to her, shaking. "I came here this afternoon and brought some lunch because there was no one home. I was just playing pirate by myself and then it began to burn and I can't swim. Leslie, I was so scared."

"It's all right, Captain Blood. You were doing fine." She kept her voice calm and under control. "This is a real adventure, isn't it?"

"I g-guess so. But adventures are nicer in books and stories, aren't they? When they are real they are kind of s-scary. W-what are we going to do? The water's dark and it seems such a long way down."

So far, only the front of the barge was on fire. "We'll wait back here and see which way it is drifting. Then, if we have to, we'll swim for the nearest bank."

"But I can't do it."

"You just hang on to me, Captain."

She stood with the small hand clutching hers feverishly. Already the wood under bare feet was hot. The fire was spreading. They'd have to swim for it. Then she halted, staring. They were drifting past the Company grounds. Two men were running from the laboratory toward a car whose motor was racing. A third man, with drawn revolver, stood beside the car. Leslie watched, petrified. Even Jack's terror faded in his absorption in the strange activities on the river bank.

There was a jolt. The barge had wedged against the center support of the covered bridge. There was a roar of flames. Somewhere men were shouting and running. Motors throbbed. A spark touched the plank beside her.

"Come on, Captain Blood." Leslie's tone was gay. "This is going to be a great adventure. Better than Robinson Crusoe. I want you to hold onto me. That's right. Take a long breath and then hold it. Here we go."

They seemed to plunge straight to the bottom of the river. Then, unexpectedly, their heads were out of water. Leslie took a long breath, filled her lungs, looked toward the bank. Two men raced toward the bridge. Saw the flames.

Halted, transfixed, in their tracks, and then ran back to pile into a car. The third man stood watching the barge. He had seen them. He must have seen them. He'd help them.

Then the man crouched, watching them. There was an infinitely furtive quality about his stealthy attitude. He was watching them sharply but he wasn't going to help. He was just—waiting.

Leslie made for shore with long, sure strokes, keeping her head under water as much as she could, endeavoring not to splash. Her feet touched ground. She looked up cautiously.

"Quiet," she said, her voice a thread of sound. "We're going ashore. Keep down and don't splash, whatever you do."

"That man," whispered Jack. "Wouldn't he help us, do you s'pose?"

Leslie was aware of such consuming rage as she had never known. A man who would frighten a child, endanger a child! She pulled herself onto the bank, drawing Jack with her. Looked around.

To the left was the burning bridge. To the right a wide open expanse led to the Company buildings, to men who ran and shouted. To safety, if she could reach it. If.

But the lurking man was too near. She'd never get away from him, hampered as she was by a small and terrified child.

Straight ahead was the cut-off that led to Route 13, and beyond that were the woods. Slowly, foot by foot, she dragged herself along the ground, pulling, cajoling Jack along with her. They would have to cross that open space. There was no help for it.

Then she said, "Now! Quick! Cross the road and run for the woods as fast as you can. Don't look back. No matter what happens, keep going!"

Jack darted ahead and she followed, trying to keep her body as a shield between the boy and the man with the revolver.

Then they were pushing through undergrowth, falling over tree stumps and the rocks that seem to push up endlessly in Connecticut soil, where within a few years a pebble seems to have grown to a boulder. The noise they made seemed terrific like an elephant crashing its way through a bamboo thicket.

"Stop," she whispered, clutching Jack's hand.

Behind them someone was floundering through the heavy underbrush. Under cover of the noise he made, Leslie pulled Jack down beside her. To judge by the thorns, they must be in a patch of brambles. But the discomfort was of small importance; all that mattered was to conceal a small boy from the man who followed.

The pursuer stumbled over some obstacle, so near him that he lashed at the blackberry bushes. He must have scraped his face, because he began to curse viciously.

"Damned near got an eye," he muttered. "I've had enough of this. But I need the girl and the kid. We've got to have 'em now."

Leslie's arm held Jack close, pressing his head against the ground. A motor throbbed. A car coming toward the cut-off to Route 13. The man hailed it.

"Why, that—" Jack whispered.

She put her fingers over his lips.

There was a murmur of words. The car was turning, backing. What on earth was it doing? It was clear off the road, at the edge of the woods, nearly upon them. Surely it wasn't going to run them down!

Headlights stabbed the undergrowth, reached like clawing fingers for the girl and the small boy. They lay prone, flattened against the ground.

"Even if they are in there, we'll never find them," a coarse voice said. "It would take a dozen men with searchlights to comb these woods. Anyhow, I don't like woods, particularly at night. Snakes and animals and things. And poison ivy, maybe. I'm allergic to poison ivy."

"You'd think these were the Maine woods with bears in them," scoffed the voice Jack had recognized. "Nothing bigger than foxes or maybe deer. They'd be more afraid of you than you are of them."

"Well, we can't wait for the girl and the kid. I'm going on. Stay and look for them yourself, if you like. But our whole timing schedule is off because of that bridge and we've got to make tracks. Even for the sake of hostages, we are risking too much."

"Okay." The familiar voice faded. A door slammed. The car turned, headed for the highway.

There was silence in the woods. Leslie barely breathed. Beside her she could feel the pounding of Jack's heart, and again she was shaken by fury that anyone should frighten a child.

Hostages!

"Can't we go now?" Jack whispered. "It's so dark in here."

"Soon. Wait a little while longer."

"But the car went away."

"I'm not sure all three men were in it."

As she strained her ears, Leslie discovered that the black silence was pricked with a score of small sounds. Whispering leaves. Snapping twigs. The scurry of unseen life. She remembered Doris's comment that the woods were alive, that at night they belonged to the animals, that human beings were intruders here.

"Snakes," the coarse strange voice had said.

A shudder shook her body. She could feel something crawling over her and told herself firmly that it was all imagination. Something struck the branch of a tree overhead and she started, then realized that it was probably a flying squirrel.

There was the faint far drone of an airplane. She wished she were safe, clear of this tangle of dark woods. High up in the limitless freedom of the open sky.

Twigs snapped and she was alert, her eyes wide, straining in the darkness. Something was moving in the undergrowth. Something—big. Her heart fluttered, steadied, missed a beat, raced and pounded in her chest.

A dead branch broke with a clap like thunder, under a man's weight. A flashlight gleamed. It played on the trees over her head, lowered. It had reached the brambles now, crept along their length. It struck her eyes, blinding her after the scented gloom of the woods.

Then she heard a low, jubilant exclamation. "Leslie, Leslie, my darling!" For a moment Donald Shaw switched the light on his own face to reassure her. He parted the brambles carefully.

"Take Jack first," she said. "I'm all right."

He picked up the small boy and in a few moments returned for her. She went into his arms, her face burrowing into his shoulder.

"Oh, Donald! Donald!"

"It's all right, my darling. All right." He laughed as the thorny stems whipped across his bare shoulders. "I do manage to put you in the most uncomfortable situations."

"I put myself in this one," she said, still clinging to him. "Oh, Donald, they might have killed Jack. Setting fire to the barge while he was on it."

Jack, with the incredible resilience of childhood, was calling impatiently, "Aw, don't be so mushy. Look, there's something going on. C'mon, Leslie."

Donald chuckled in his relief. "We're coming, but it's all over now."

"Someone set that fire," Leslie said.

"I know," he told her grimly. "When I realized you were on that burning barge, I nearly went crazy."

"You're soaking wet."

"So are you," he reminded her. "That's a very wet river."

"You went in after us?"

"Of course. But Charlie Turgen saw you dive over the side with the boy. He tried to reach you when you came ashore and he was knocked out for his pains. Some guy was trying to stop you. I've been hunting for you and going slowly out of my mind. I was afraid they would reach you first, try to hold you as hostages."

"That's what they intended. Something must have gone wrong with their plans."

"It was Jim Mason after us," Jack said. "I heard his voice. I told Paul Logan all along he was a pirate but not a usial one."

"Not usial at all," Donald agreed.

"How right you were, Captain Blood," Leslie said. "We'll make Paul eat his words."

"So it was Mason," Donald said.

"I believe you knew it all the time," Leslie accused him. "What's happening at the laboratory?"

"You'll find out later. Your father can tell you. Right now I'm taking you both home before you get pneumonia."

"My father's at the laboratory?"

Donald laughed suddenly. "Practically the whole village is there."

"And the formula?"

"Later," he said firmly. "Can you walk with those bare feet or shall I carry you?"

He settled Leslie and Jack in the Volkswagen and flashed his light in an arc three times. Lieutenant Varelli came up breathlessly.

"Are they okay?"

"All present and accounted for, though slightly damp," Donald said cheerfully.

"You are to go straight through Route 13. The roadblocks have been lifted." The lieutenant gave a boyish laugh. "Just got word. They ran straight into our arms! Quite a surprise party. Our boys gave them a real welcome." He touched his cap in a salute. "Good night."

As Donald let in the clutch, Leslie said, "Why the fancy salute?"

"Just high spirits, I guess. You're shivering. I'll get you home as fast as I can." He turned on the car heater. "Oh, Leslie, my poor darling! First I nearly overturn you in a sidecar, and then I find you all wrapped up in a blackberry bush. Now I've put you in a regular steam laundry. I'll leave you at home so you can get out of those wet clothes, and take Jack on to Web Rock."

She was half asleep with exhaustion and reaction when the car stopped at the Blake house. In the back seat Jack was sleeping soundly, undisturbed by the puddle of water in which he lay. Donald took Leslie's arm, guided her stumbling feet to the door, rang the bell.

"Good night, my dearest." He kissed her lips lightly and ran back to the car.

Agatha opened the door, looked at the girl, her wet slip clinging to her, water dripping from her hair, a deep scratch across one cheek.

"Leslie!" She drew her in, took her upstairs, turned on hot water and helped the stumbling, weary girl into the tub, without fuss or question. She had to awaken her to get her out of the tub and into bed.

"All right?" she asked anxiously.

Leslie turned her cheek on the pillow and dropped fathoms deep into sleep.

THAT night the heat wave was broken by a drenching rain, which finally extinguished the last smoldering embers of the fire. The covered bridge had been consumed; only the concrete supports remained. The barge had burned down to the waterline.

The downpour soaked the weary members of the Volunteer Fire Department as they turned back to their homes. It drenched the men who, for the second time, were nailing boards over a broken window in the laboratory. It washed like waves over the windshields of patrol cars as they brought their sullen captives to the state police barracks.

But for the most part, the people of Claytonville awakened, listened in relief to the cooling promise of the rain, and turned on their sides to sleep again. And there were some who did not hear it at all.

At Web Rock, Captain Blood slept restlessly, battling with a nightmare in which a strange man chased him through deep woods, with danger lurking on either side.

In another room, Doris dropped off to sleep, hoping that Paul had got home safely from the fire. He was, of course, a member of the Volunteer Fire Department.

In still another room, Jane stared into the dark, thinking about the time fuse she had lighted for the next day. She pictured herself, the center of attention, in a white dress and a big white hat, unveiling the sculpture that represented Douglas Clayton's heroic action. She hoped arrangements had been made for the metropolitan press to be there. *Life* might even send a photographer. She was very photogenic.

At the Blake house, Leslie slept deeply and in her sleep she smiled to herself.

Agatha, who had watched silently beside her stepdaughter's bed, fearful of a rise in temperature, touched the girl's cool skin and went quietly back to her own room. She glanced at her watch. Nearly one o'clock. Corliss hadn't come home.

She wasn't tired at all. She might as well wait up for him.

She settled herself in a rocking chair by the window and took up her vigil. Corliss! When he did return, he'd want her to be waiting, to hear about what had happened. She rocked contentedly, while rain beat on the windows and on the garden, soaked into the dry ground, reached the thirsty roots of trees.

In a narrow hospital bed, Oliver Harrison stirred uneasily, opened his eyes. The nurse, who had been watching the handsome profile with admiration, smiled at him. He felt the lump on his head, frowning.

"I am your special Mrs. Lamb. You've been x-rayed. Nothing but a nasty knock," she assured him. "I understand you were quite the hero of the occasion, Mr. Harrison."

He gave her his warm smile. "Only did my job," he said modestly.

"Mr. Blake called up. Very anxious about you he was. He couldn't get away but he'll be around to see you in the morning."

"I'll be up and around in the morning," Harrison assured her. "It takes more than I got to put me out of the running."

He spoke lightly, but the nurse had an uneasy feeling that he could be a dangerous man. He was obviously consumed with anger about the knockout blow he had received. She was aware of a stirring of sympathy for the man who had attacked him. Mr. Harrison was not one to leave a score unsettled.

"What happened after I was brought here?" he asked.

"Now, Mr. Harrison, you'll know all about it in the morning when Mr. Blake comes. You mustn't get excited. If you need a sleeping pill, I'm to give you one."

"Sleep! I can't sleep until I know."

He saw the quiet determination on her face when he raised his voice in irritation. This wasn't the way to handle a woman who was accustomed to dealing competently with the vagaries of the ill, trained to disregard the unreason of people who were fretful.

"Please, Mrs. Lamb!" He changed his tactics. "Tell me about it and then I'll sleep like a baby."

She responded to his cajoling manner with a pleased little laugh. "Well, all right then. It's the most excitement Claytonville ever had. An attempt was made, as you know, to steal the formula the Company has been working on. As a distraction from the burglary, fire was set to the barge at the old Clayton place, the Blake place it is now. Of course, you know better than anyone, you saved the formula. Then, after that, everything went wrong."

"What happened?" he asked sharply.

"Now you must not get excited," she said soothingly. "Well, the barge broke loose. It was supposed to burn right there and keep the firemen and the police on the other side of the river. Instead, it got away and jammed into the covered bridge. The bridge is gone, of course. Such a pity. People used to come from all over to photograph it or to paint it. Anyhow, the fire on the bridge cut off the line of retreat. Instead of getting straight back into the village, the criminals had to take Route 13 eight miles before they could cross the river. The state police had been prepared for something happening, so roadblocks were set up."

"They caught the men?"

The nurse heard the tension in his voice. "Oh, dear, yes," she said reassuringly. She put her hand on Harrison's pulse. "You must not worry any more," she told him cheerfully. "Everything is under control."

At the Fox and Rabbit, Felice Allen, in pale green pajamas and matching satin mules, paced the floor of her room. Her red hair was like a flame, her narrow green eyes were shadowed, cigarette butts had piled up in the ashtray. The room was blue with smoke, but she could not open the window because of the driving force of the rain.

Why didn't he call her as he had promised? What had happened? She had heard the hoarse toots of the fire alarm, the clang of the hook and ladder, and had watched private cars dart past toward the covered bridge, lights blinking. She had seen the flames as the bridge caught fire.

Something had gone wrong. She lighted another cigarette. Listened. The fire was over, the weary firefighters had left, there was only the steady drum of the rain. Through the water on the windowpane she could make out a couple of street lamps, the dim lights inside drugstore and grocery store that burned all night. Nothing else. The deadly quiet of the village. How she hated the place!

She longed with all her heart for the ceaseless roar of New York traffic, the tooting of boats signaling in the East River, the lights that never went out, the sense of life, feverish life, going on around her. In New York she'd be catching a new night spot show, sketching some celebrity's dress, or making notes about jewelry or an evening bag. She had even done a moving column once on what jeweled pillboxes could do for a woman's personality, particularly if she carried pills in pretty pastel shades. There was some sense in that. Some drama.

She lighted another cigarette. For weeks she had dragged

out the time here. They had better be worth it. She made up her mind that they would be worth it. Someone would pay for those weeks of boredom and pay heavily.

She put out the half-smoked cigarette. A sick conviction struck her. He wasn't going to call. She switched out her light and lay sleepless in bed, listening to the relentless beat of the rain.

*   *   *

At the state police barracks, lights were blazing. The forces of law never go off duty. The lieutenant, as alert as though he had not already put in eighteen hours of duty, reached for the thick cup of coffee a trooper brought him.

"Thanks. But what I'd really prefer would be a three-course meal."

The trooper grinned. "I'm thinking of taking up cooking in my time off. If any."

The sergeant who had been making notes leaned back and flexed his cramped fingers.

Varelli sipped his coffee and then looked at the two prisoners in front of him. A third man sat on a chair across the room, his head sunk on his chest. Corliss Blake sat quietly, without making any comment.

"Well," the lieutenant said, "looks to me as though we've got the whole story." He turned to a trooper. "You've sent on those fingerprints?"

"Yes, sir. We ought to get an answer some time tomorrow."

"Okay," one of the two men standing in front of his desk said in resignation, "the prints are on record."

"You've done time?"

"Two years. Armed hold-up. Gus here was in Sing Sing at the same time. Second offender."

"You—" snarled Gus.

The first man shrugged. "Look, they've got us cold on that. No point in lying about it. They'll dig up the records. Only thing is that they haven't a single thing on us this time but smashing a window and setting it up to look like a gang job."

"We didn't steal anything," Gus pointed out hopefully.

Varelli grinned. "That's right. You didn't. There's another matter, of course. Arson. Burning the barge, the covered bridge."

Both exconvicts turned to glare at Jim Mason, who did not lift his head.

"That was his idea. Trust an amateur."

"How did Mason get onto you two?"

"We knew a buddy of his in Sing Sing. Mason's brother-in-law. Dead now. Guy named Allen. Forger."

"Okay. Take them away," the lieutenant said.

A trooper nodded toward a door. "Get going," he said. The two prisoners shuffled out without a word.

Varelli finished his coffee, taking his time. "Well, Mason?"

"Look," the accountant said desperately, "it was an accident. Just chance. I was helping fight the fire. See? And then the firemen got on the job so I wasn't needed. I hailed this car for a hitch back. Never saw them before in my life." He mopped perspiration from his forehead with shaking hands. "Nor a word of truth in what they were saying."

"Just asked for a lift, is that it?" Varelli said pleasantly.

Jim Mason nodded in relief. "That's it."

"But why didn't you use your own car? It's still in the parking lot at the Company, and I'm darned if I can see how you fought the fire from this side of the river."

Mason stared at him blankly. Moistened dry lips.

"Where did you work before you came here, Mason?"

"Uh—accountant with a printing firm in New York. Gone out of business now. Then, before that, a firm in Cleveland. But—"

"Let me guess." Varelli was still pleasant. "It's gone out of business, too."

"Well, it does happen," Mason said sullenly.

"It sure does. But how about your job in the accounting department of the Gypton Company? Did that just slip your mind?"

The freckles stood out against the pallor of Jim Mason's face. "I've got nothing more to say until I see a lawyer."

"Tough luck on you that Harrison was guarding that formula," Varelli commented. "How much did Gypton offer you for it?"

Somewhat to his own surprise, Jim Mason refused to tell him.

THE morning of the Clayton Festival dawned bright and clear. The day seemed to have been freshly washed by the rain of the night before. A light breeze and a warm sun were rapidly drying the bunting.

Corliss Blake and Agatha, after a sleepless night, spent a couple of frantic hours making telephone calls. A meeting was to be held in the Town Hall at one o'clock. The village was filled with wild rumors. The formula had been saved. No, it had been stolen. Oliver Harrison—such a handsome man, my dear!—had been shot. No, he had been stabbed. Five exconvicts had been caught after a running gun battle in which at least three had been killed. Corliss Blake had been held all night at the state police barracks for questioning. He was under arrest.

Do you really think . . . of course not, such a nice family, but you can't tell me there's not something behind this. Where there's smoke there's fire.

Long before noon, a crowd had begun to gather in front of the Town Hall. The local constable was helpless to cope with the confusion. Fortunately, the state police were on hand, though the original plans had not called for them to appear before three o'clock when the parade was scheduled to start.

"Keep moving, please," they repeated monotonously. "Sorry, no parking on the Green. Keep moving. You can't—oh, it's you, Mr. Blake. Okay. Go right in. We'll take care of your car for you. Hi, Joe, park this, will you?"

Corliss Blake stood back to let his wife and daughter precede him into the Town Hall. Agatha walked with her usual unhurried dignity, Leslie with a confident smile at her father and a proud tilt to her head. They went through the curious throng without a look to either side.

Leslie and Agatha found seats at one side, where some of the big tables, already set for supper, had been hastily removed. It was an excellent vantage point, as they could obtain a clear view of the room without seeming to stare around them.

Corliss mounted the three steps to the platform. Slowly people began to filter in. Now and then, Leslie took a quick glance at them. The chemists had arrived practically in a body and they filled one row, except for Donald Shaw. He was standing alone against the wall at the back. For a moment his eyes met Leslie's and held them, and her heart warmed as though he had clasped her hand.

Some members of the Clayton Festival Committee had arrived now. She recognized Mrs. Hastings, who for some reason was holding a large cake with a sticky icing, apparently under the impression that she was supposed to be bringing food for the supper. Miss Eustace's booming voice dominated the room, then dropped away as Felice Allen, very white, narrow green eyes as hard as emeralds, came in and sat at the end of a row.

Doris and Jane arrived with Paul. Doris waved to Leslie. Jane was looking around her eagerly.

Oliver Harrison, very pale and looking very brave, came slowly into the room and then, without hesitation, went up to take a seat on the platform beside Corliss Blake. Leslie saw the astonished arc of her father's heavy eyebrows, then the beginning of a sardonic smile in his eyes. However, he maintained his gravity, and spoke a quiet greeting to his head chemist.

Watching Oliver, Leslie knew that this was his moment of triumph. He had saved the formula and, consequently, the Company; he intended to strike while the iron was hot, to wrest every possible advantage he could from the situation.

There was a little stir and a half-embarrassed murmur as Jim Mason came in, accompanied by a state trooper. They sat side by side. Leslie noticed now that several troopers, quiet, unostentatious, but alert, were stationed at strategic intervals, and her heart quickened. Something was going to happen.

Lieutenant Varelli had been standing at the door, talking to someone who was out of line with Leslie's vision. Then, with a quick look around, he nodded, let the man with whom he had been talking come in, and issued a lowtoned order. The door closed with a curiously final sound.

Leslie found her heart was pounding, a wild runaway out of control. She looked at the stranger to whom Varelli had been talking. He was a big burly man with heavy pepper-and-salt hair and a barrel chest. She had never seen him before.

With the closing of the door Jim Mason had looked up, straight into the face of the newcomer. He gave a startled gasp and then seemed to gather himself together, to shrink. He did not raise his eyes again.

Varelli made his way up to the platform, glanced curiously at Harrison, exchanged looks with Corliss Blake, nodded, and took the third chair.

Corliss Blake rose slowly. "Many of you must wonder why I have called this meeting," he began, his voice easy and relaxed. Insensibly, Leslie felt her heartbeat slow and steady. Her father looked down at the attentive faces. Unexpectedly, he smiled.

"I'm sorry to disappoint you. Judging by some of the rumors I have heard this morning, the truth is going to seem rather flat and undramatic. But I wanted the people in Claytonville to know the truth. The Company and the people of this community have long belonged to each other. You are entitled to know what has been going on, especially because, in a way, all of you are concerned, whether employees or not. The covered bridge that was destroyed last night was your property. You have a right to know what was behind that wanton destruction."

He paused to drink a sip of water. "Almost all of you know that several years ago the Company had the privilege of acquiring a brilliant young research chemist, a man named Fosdick, who, unfortunately, died before he could realize the full extent and the value of the new formula he had begun to develop. After his death, we were again fortunate in gaining the highly competent services of Mr. Oliver Harrison, who has played a large part in perfecting the new formula."

Corliss Blake looked around him, as though at a circle of his closest friends, his tone relaxed and pleasant. "Now, of course, in the highly competitive industrial age in which we live, there was not much hope that we could develop so revolutionary a concept without rumors reaching the trade. In time, they did. Then, a more serious thing happened. It became apparent that some, at least, of the data which we had hoped to keep secret had reached one of our competitors. Somewhere," his voice hardened, "we had a traitor in the Company."

No one moved. No one seemed to breathe.

"That was a bitter thing to me. The Company and its welfare had been left in my hands by the death of Douglas Clayton and I wanted to do my best for them. Many of the employees are second, third, even, in a few cases, fourth generations of Claytonville people to work for the Company. To suspect them of treachery was a painful thing. The only alternative was to scrutinize more carefully the background of the few newcomers. When my point of view became apparent, several things happened. One was an attempt to provide me with a fall guy, a patsy, I believe it is called. Having a natural disinclination to follow the carrot so invitingly held before my nose like a patient donkey—"

There was a little ripple of laughter. Only Oliver Harrison failed to look amused. His jaw tightened, his air of determination was more apparent. But Corliss Blake did not observe it. Since he had greeted Harrison on his arrival, he had not once looked at him.

"So, the second thing happened. Pressures began to be made on me to resign from the Company. Again, I refused to be a tool in the hands of other people. I held to my course."

There was a scattering of applause. Agatha looked at Leslie and their hands touched briefly.

"And then, the third thing happened. A window in the laboratory was smashed, someone ran into Mrs. Turgen, an employee on night duty, knocked her out and stabbed her. If she had not received immediate help, she might well have bled to death."

Blake paused for another sip of water. There was a curious alteration in his manner. Both Leslie and Agatha noticed it and looked at each other questioningly.

"There have been a great many rumors afloat about that attempt to steal the formula. But this is not the time to deal with rumors. The essential thing is that it failed. So we come at last to the events of last night when a second attempt was made to rob the laboratory."

There was a buzz of whispered comment and he raised his hand, waiting for silence. "That attempt, as I have said, involved not only the Company but the whole community, because, in the course of a long-planned but blundering operation, the covered bridge, which belongs to you all and has served the community for more than a hundred and fifty years, was destroyed. But, for all its destructive aspects, the attempt was a complete failure. Today, the two exconvicts who engineered the scheme, on behalf of a competitor, are under arrest. And the formula is safe."

There was a wave of applause, which he had some difficulty in checking.

"On Monday morning," he said, raising his voice to dominate the confusion, "the Clayton Textile Company will announce its new product to the trade. Within a few years, the organization should be one of the great ones in the field, perhaps in the whole country. We have only begun to guess as yet at its potentialities. And now, with my task done, the time has come for me to step down, to place in better hands the fortunes and the welfare of the Company we all love."

There was a moment's silence, then several voices began to speak at once. It was Wilcox who shouted, "We want Blake for president."

The crowd took up the chant: "We want Blake! We want Blake! We want Blake!"

Agatha squeezed Leslie's hand convulsively, but Leslie was watching her father, puzzled. What was he really trying to do? Oliver Harrison stirred in his chair, jaws clamped, eyes burning.

Blake smiled. "Thank you, my friends. But there is, I believe, someone else whom you must thank—the man who saved the formula last night. Our head chemist, Oliver Harrison."

He gestured toward Harrison and then, without warning, sat down, leaving the floor to him.

Oliver stood up slowly, stood up to face a polite but silent group. Anger tore at him. He had achieved what he wanted, but where was his triumph?

He spoke with smiling assurance, as though he had received an ovation instead of this mute, apathetic acceptance.

"Thank you, Mr. Blake, for your kind words. In saving the formula, I was only doing my small part for the Company. And a bump on the head is a little price to pay in frustrating the attempts to rob us of our achievement."

He smiled, a rueful expression on his good-looking face, making light of his accident. Still there was no response, there were no answering smiles.

"Mr. Blake has showed his usual indulgence," Oliver said, an edge to his voice, "by trying to protect his own employees, or, shall I say, his own employee, his own choice, from complicity in last night's burglary. But," again he smiled, trying to win over his hostile audience, "I'm afraid I'm not quite so indulgent. I'm the man who was knocked out and I have a long memory. The man who struck me, the man who engineered the attempt to steal the formula, was Donald Shaw!"

A collective gasp was followed by an excited murmur. Somewhere in the room there was a disturbance. Nors Swensen was trying to get away from the firm hold of a state trooper. Charlie Turgen was forcing his way belligerently through the crowd.

And then a voice said clearly, "That's a lie!"

Jim Mason stood up, the trooper beside him, keeping ominous pace with him as the accountant walked up to the platform.

"You can take back that lie, Oliver! I'm the one who knocked you out. You knew that at the time."

"The man's crazy," Harrison said, his voice rising, out of control.

Lieutenant Varelli spoke for the first time. "All right, Mason. Let's hear your story. I thought you'd talk if you saw Harrison ready to take over the Company."

"You bet I'll talk. I was working for—well, Mr. Blake calls 'em 'a competitor.' That's good enough for me. They wanted the formula and offered a nice price for it. The offer sounded all right to me, ten thousand dollars and expenses if I could work out a method to get hold of it without arousing suspicion. Well, I got a job here and contacted some guys who were friends of my sister's first husband, Allen. We figured out how to play it but we didn't know chemistry or how to recognize the formula if we saw it. We needed a trained man. That's where Oliver Harrison came in. He's my sister's second husband. She always picks crooks."

"*Is?*" Blake interrupted sharply.

"Sure. She keeps her first husband's name because that's when she made her professional reputation. Felice Allen. She was in it, too. Harrison was going to be finger man and those torpedoes I met through Felice could help stage a job that would look like an outside one and take the pressure off Oliver."

"Can't you see he's lying?" Harrison protested. He wiped wet hands on his handkerchief.

"Go on, Mason," Varelli said.

"Well, Oliver came up here and after a while he began to get ideas. He didn't want to sell the formula. He wanted to keep it, become president of the Company and marry the boss's daughter."

"But he had a wife," Blake's voice was under control, but his hands clenched when he thought of Harrison's attitude toward Leslie.

"He had a wife, all right." Felice Allen was on her feet now, her red head high in defiance, manner insolent, eyes hard and glittering. "Not that I want him, you understand. I was going to give him his divorce. But I wanted to be sure I'd get a fair cut in alimony. So I came here to look around. It took me weeks to figure that Oliver had changed the program. That's why Jim staged the first robbery. To warn Oliver that we meant business. He was going to sell me out. The way he's sold Jim out. So now Jim takes the rap and Oliver takes the presidency."

"I saved the formula," Oliver said. "That's my answer to this nonsense."

"That interests me," Varelli said. "If you were innocent of any complicity, if you didn't know about last night's plan, how did you happen to have the formula in your pocket?"

"Laugh that off," Jim Mason snarled.

"And we have a couple of items for you to laugh off, Mason," Varelli said smoothly. "Conspiracy. Breaking and entering. Assault with a deadly weapon. Arson. The near murder of Mrs. Turgen. The attempt to kidnap Miss Blake and Jack Williams to hold as hostages when your original plans fell through. Take him away."

They took him away. For a long moment Felice Allen and Oliver Harrison stared at each other. Then she smiled. "I told you that you overrated yourself and underrated other people, my sweet. You met your match when you tried to undermine Donald Shaw. When you met him, you met your Waterloo."

And then Jane Williams moved. She came forward slowly, her hand on the arm of the burly stranger. When they were directly below the platform, she said, her voice high and sweet and clear, "Will you please tell us who you are?"

"My name is Donald Shaw."

There was a collective gasp.

"Until today I was a chemist with the Gypton Company. I resigned because I don't like their methods."

"Is there a Donald Shaw who is related to you?"

"My nephew was named for me."

Jane smiled. "Also employed by Gypton?"

"Also employed by Gypton."

"I knew it," Jane cried triumphantly. "From the very beginning I knew it!"

Every face had turned toward Donald Shaw, who remained leaning casually against the wall, serene and composed.

"Well?" Jane demanded. "Is he your nephew?"

The burly man shook his head, as he followed her eyes to the tall man who looked steadily back at him, half smiling. "That is not my nephew; Donald Shaw was killed in the Korean War."

"Then who is this man?"

The man from Gypton began to grin. He opened his lips. Before he could speak, Lieutenant Varelli intervened.

"I think I can answer that question. I've checked his fingerprints with those the army had and also his other—credentials. That is Douglas Clayton."

xxii

In the excitement that followed, the crowd swept between Leslie and Donald—Douglas Clayton—and bore him away with them in triumph. When she had caught her breath, Leslie looked back toward the platform. She saw on Oliver Harrison's face an expression of utter, bitter defeat. He scarcely noticed when Lieutenant Varelli touched his arm. He accompanied him almost listlessly through a side door.

And then at last Corliss Blake came down the steps to join his wife and daughter. He had had weeks of mounting anxiety and had just passed a sleepless night, but there was a look of delight on his face that transformed it. At last, he could turn over an alien burden and responsibility, restore property and position to which he had never felt entitled, and he could give them back to their rightful owner.

He smiled at his wife and daughter. He did not attempt to make himself heard above the uproar in the Town Hall. He led them toward the side door. A state police car was moving away. On the back seat, Oliver Harrison and Felice Allen sat side by side.

A trooper saw Blake and held up his hands. "I'll have your car around here in just a minute." He grinned. "The village has gone mad. And the Clayton Festival to be held today! There's never been anything like this before."

"Good heaven," Agatha exclaimed, "we can't leave, Leslie! We've got to get the Town Hall in shape again for the supper."

If she had been asked whether she was capable of any exertion in her state of turmoil, Leslie would have uttered an emphatic "No." But under Agatha's skillful guidance, Leslie and Doris and Paul Logan found members of the Committee, cut them out of the pack, and set them to work. Within an hour order had been restored and the tables had been put back and reset.

"Jeepers," Doris said at last. "Did you see Jane's face? Jeepers!"

It was curious, Leslie thought, that in all the tumult of emotions she had experienced since the identity of Douglas Clayton had been revealed, she had not remembered that Jane Williams had been his great love. In a blinding flash she understood the full extent of his sacrifice, the immensity of his love for the woman who had just tried so tenaciously to expose and disgrace him publicly.

She was silent while Doris and Paul drove her and Agatha back to their house, where Corliss Blake was sleeping.

"Get some rest, dear, before you change for the Festival," Agatha said. "You're terribly white. I'll have Rosie bring a tray up to your room. You—you must look your prettiest this afternoon, you know."

Leslie managed a wavering, uncertain smile. In her room she sank down on the chaise longue. Her head, she thought, resembled a beehive. There was such a buzz of confusion that she couldn't seem to think straight. Donald Shaw— Douglas Clayton.

Rosie came in with a tray. "Cold soup and some chicken sandwiches," she said. "Now be sure to eat it all. My, I can't get over it. Mr. Clayton alive and home again!"

Leslie looked at the long narrow ivory box on the tray with a piece of notepaper wrapped around it.

"What's this?"

"A messenger just brought it."

Leslie opened the paper. She had never seen the handwriting before but she recognized it at once.

"My darling, these are the Clayton emeralds. They told me at the bank your father had never taken them out of the vault. They are yours now. Wear them for me. I love you with all my heart. Douglas."

She opened the ivory box, looked at the necklace, her breath catching as she realized its great beauty.

She closed the box gently and put it to one side.

It was nearly three o'clock when she opened it again. Dressed in drifting yellow powdered with gold flakes, copper glints in her short brown curls, her soft mouth brave with its vivid lipstick, she clasped the necklace around her throat.

"Good heavens!" Agatha said from the doorway. "How magnificent. Can those stones possibly be real?"

"They're the Clayton emeralds," Leslie told her. "He— Donald—Douglas—sent them to me."

Agatha said, "I don't think I'm going to keep my daughter very long." She added, "I'm so glad."

Leslie laughed. "What a terrible way of putting it."

"Oh, dear!" Agatha joined in the laughter. "But you know what I mean."

There was a sound of drums in the distance and Corliss Blake called up the stairs, "The parade's about to start! I wish my girls would get a move on. I have to welcome the Governor when he arrives and the man is a demon for punctuality."

When they reached the grandstand, it was apparent that not only all of Claytonville but of the neighboring communities had gathered on the Green. Corliss Blake went forward to welcome the Governor, who was just getting out of his car.

"This is kind of you, Governor."

The Governor shook hands warmly. "This is my son Frank, Mr. Blake. When he heard over the radio that Douglas Clayton had turned up, alive and well, he insisted on coming along. Is it true?"

"It's true," Blake assured him. "But I don't know where Clayton is. I haven't caught sight of him since the crowd swept him out of the Town Hall this morning. I understand they carried him on their shoulders up to the top of the Green before he could stop them."

"He's on his way." Nors Swensen came up to the speakers' stand. "I just left him at the Fox and Rabbit."

Leslie leaned forward. "Mr. Swensen, I believe you knew all the time who he was."

Nors grinned. "I recognized him the first time I laid eyes on him. Not his looks, of course, but his ways. Why, I practically brought Doug up. Right then and there I suspected that Harrison was trying to bait a trap and use Doug for the cheese. He needed someone he could set up as a patsy if anything went wrong for him. Doug and I have been working together ever since. At least, we did until the first burglary. Then I figured things were getting out of hand and Doug might be up against it and need a little help. So I had a private talk with Lieutenant Varelli, who checked Doug's fingerprints with the War Department. The guys down there knew he was alive, of course. Then Varelli got onto Dr. John Forsyth, who told him the rest. Ten years of operations to put him together again. The doctor wanted to carry him and his expenses all that time but Doug made him agree to let him pay it back. That's all he meant to ask from his estate. Doug," he cleared his throat, "is quite a guy."

"But why?" Blake asked. "Why did he keep out of sight all those years? Why did he take the name of Donald Shaw?"

"He knew Shaw in Korea. They were both chemists so they had a kind of bond. Then Shaw was killed the day Doug took that machine-gun nest, so, when Doug knew what he was up against, he took Shaw's identity. Except he wrote to Shaw's uncle and told him the truth. Then they got together later on the attempt to steal the formula. Shaw's an all right guy and didn't like any part of that deal. I kind of expect that Doug will give him Harrison's job."

"I still don't understand," Blake admitted.

"Well, there wasn't much of Doug left after the Tower Heights offensive. Not much hope for him until he was shipped back here and got in touch with Dr. Forsyth, an old family friend."

"Forsyth!" the Governor exclaimed. "The great plastic surgeon?"

"Yup."

"The man is supposed to be a miracle worker."

"He set to work building Doug a new face and fixed up all the things that were wrong with him."

"But I still—" Blake persisted.

"Don't you see, Dad," Leslie told him, "he never intended to come back. Because of Jane. He loved her and she would have hated to marry him when anything was wrong. So he—just disappeared. For her sake. I think that was his real, his biggest sacrifice."

"Oh!"

At that cry, Leslie turned to look at Jane, beautiful in the white dress and hat that she had selected for the unveiling ceremony. She was staring at Leslie with the strangest expression on her face. Incredibly, she looked pleased.

"Did he—did Doug—do that for me? How wonderful of him! How perfectly marvelous. When I see him I'll—" She broke off, her eyes on the emeralds around Leslie's slim throat. Her exultant smile faded. "The Clayton emeralds," she said. "I—see. I don't think I'll stay for the unveiling. Can someone replace me?" She turned and walked swiftly away.

"Poor thing," Agatha said. "I think she still expected to make things right with Douglas Clayton."

"Ten years," Leslie reminded her, and there was no sympathy in the girl's voice. "Ten years of exile and unhappiness and pain. Ten years that we've got to make up to him, somehow."

There were scattered cheers that swelled to a deep, heart-shaking roar. "Clayton! Clayton!"

Then the crowd opened, and a beaming Lieutenant Varelli pushed his way through, followed by a somewhat disheveled

Douglas Clayton. They mounted the steps to the place where
the Governor was waiting. The latter held out his hand. He
spoke into the microphone so that his voice reached the
crowd:

"As Mayor Walker once said to Colonel Lindbergh, 'If
you've brought a letter of introduction, you don't need it.'"

Again there was the deep-throated sound of the crowd
roaring "Welcome home, Clayton!"

The Governor's son pounded Douglas Clayton's shoulder.
"Doug! Doug! Thank God, you made it!"

Down the street came the sound of drums, the shrill voice
of a fife, the steady beat of marching feet. The Clayton
Festival had begun.

*   *   *

The last drum majorette had gone by with twirling baton,
the Veterans of Foreign Wars had drawn up to attention,
the Governor had delivered his oration, hastily revised to ap-
ply to this strange return from the dead. Nors Swensen, a
glint in his eye, was completely master of the occasion. Whatever moving reminiscences he had originally marshaled were
discarded, and he told a series of rollicking stories about
Douglas Clayton's boyhood, with a cheerful impudence that
helped to relieve the overcharged emotionalism that had been
built up.

It was Agatha Blake who completed the ceremony on the
Green by unveiling the bas-relief of the Tower Heights offensive.

"This loving tribute to Douglas Clayton's magnificent action is the work of," she smiled at Corliss, "our daughter,
Leslie Blake."

Douglas looked at it for a long time in silence.

"My God," he breathed softly, "what have I ever done to
deserve all this?"

Then came a shouted demand of "Speech! Speech!"

Douglas, shaking his head helplessly, turned to Corliss
Blake in mute appeal. The latter's voice was picked up by the
loudspeakers.

"I must say to you what was said to George Washington
when he received his first public ovation. 'Sit down, Mr.
Washington. Your modesty is equaled only by your bravery
and that exceeds any words of mine.'"

After a concerted rush to try to shake Douglas's hand, the
crowd dispersed to meet again at seven for the supper in the
Town Hall.

Then Corliss Blake turned to Douglas. "My house," he said,

"is most truly yours. Won't you let me send to the Fox and Rabbit for your luggage, and come home with us?"

"Mr. Blake, please understand that I have not returned here because I wanted to put you out of the house or the Company. I had to come to find out how things were being handled. But I—you've done a swell job."

"Look here," Blake said in some alarm, "you're not going to leave me stuck with the business. I've done my best for you and now I'm eager to be on my own. Agatha and I have more plans that we can live long enough to carry out. Do come home."

"Later, then, if I may. It's been a—pretty staggering experience. And I have some important unfinished business."

He stood looking down at Leslie. Without a word she held out her hand. He took it in his own and led her away from the Green, down toward the deserted shady path that followed the bank of the river.

At last he said, "Do you understand now?"

"I think so. When you discovered the extent of your injuries, you stayed away to spare Jane. You let Douglas Clayton die. You meant him to stay dead."

"About Jane," he said, "I'd like to explain."

She smiled at him. "Faith," she reminded him, "and without questions."

"No, I want you to understand. I was just a kid and she was so lovely. I adored her. No, that isn't strictly true. I fell in love with an illusion, one of those strange rootless infatuations like those in *A Midsummer-Night's Dream*. And when I came back, though I knew she had married immediately after I was reported missing, though I'd heard you say that she had stuck my pictures away in an old trunk, though I was literally dead for her, she—well, I'd been dreaming of her for ten years.

"That Sunday morning when I saw her at the Fox and Rabbit she was more beautiful than ever and the sight of me disturbed her in some way, though heaven knows that Dr. Forsyth had rebuilt my whole face, bit by bit. And I was terribly shaken.

"Then, little by little, I began to see her through the the eyes of a mature man: her shallowness, her selfishness, her—emptiness. And before I knew it, the whole moonlit mirage had faded away in the bright sunlight that is you."

His hand tightened on hers, they walked slowly along the path, in and out of the heavy shade, in and out of sunlight, a tall man and a slight girl, with the world ahead of them. She looked up at him, saw the bitter lines fade from his face, saw that he was no longer looking back at horror and pain and disillusionment, but looking ahead with happiness and eagerness and hope.

"Tell me," he said suddenly, "is it still true? Surprised by joy?"

"I am too deeply happy to have any words for it," she told him.

"When will you marry me?"

"Whenever you like."

"At once then," he said and something in his voice brought soft color to her cheeks. "There's no time to be lost. Perhaps I may have only another fifty years or so of you. I can't afford to waste a single minute of it."

On a bench under the trees they sat looking at the river. What they said to each other has been said a million times before, will be said a million times again. But like spring it carries its own eternal magic.

His arm held her close and she rested her head on his shoulder.

"Douglas," she said.

"Yes, darling?"

"I was just practicing. It's still so new to me."

"We'll ask your father to stay on until after our honeymoon," he said. "Then—will the old house suit you or would you rather have a newer one?"

She thought for a fleeting moment of Oliver Harrison and the big establishment he had planned that would be an "attention-getter."

"Anywhere, so long as I am with you," she confessed. The dimple flashed.

"At least you must choose where you'd like to spend your honeymoon."

"I don't honestly know, Douglas. What about you?"

"I don't care. Wherever it is, it will be the Garden of Eden with the sun shining on it."

The clock on the high church tower bonged seven times. "Good lord, we're going to be late!" He caught her hand and they ran along the river path, out of a patch of shade, into the sunlight.